D0050965

Oh, right! I had to walk to the **traffic light**! I took the second street on the left, then the third on the right, and then the first on the left. I crossed the **bridge** and counted **twenty-three-and-a-half** steps toward the **GORGONZOLA** cheese billboard.

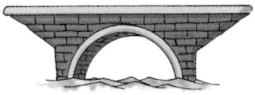

I counted **fourteen** steps toward the phone booth. There was the **CLOCK**! After counting **SEVEN** steps, I found myself in front of the pizzeria. I went in. The owner winked at me. **HOW STRANGE!** I went into the **BATHROOM**, exited through the small window, and climbed over the low wall. I walked for exactly **thirty** seconds toward

RESTROOMS

the shoe store. I went around the corner, and I found a small black door with a sign that read **DO NOT ENTER**.

I opened the door using the MYSTERIOUS key, and I found myself in an ALLEY. I took the first right, then the second left, then the third right, and finally turned into a YARD. There, I found the Dumpster. I took off the lid. Ugh! **What a stench!** I pinched my nose and climbed inside. But as soon as I got in, the bottom gave out and I fell into what seemed to be an endless dark TUNNEL.

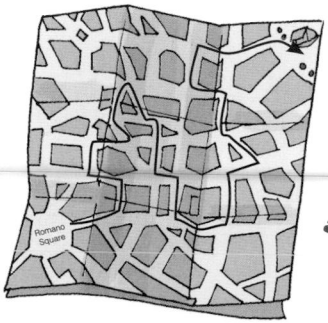

I shouted as loudly as I could:

"HEEEEEEEEEEEEEEEEEELP!"

"HEEEEEEEEEEEEEEEEELP!"

Everything around me was **PITCH-BLACK**. I fell for what seemed like forever. Was it seconds, minutes, or hours? I couldn't tell. I only know that at one point I **BOUNCED** onto some sort of trampoline. Boing! I bounced! And bounced! And bounced!

A steel clamp grabbed my tail. Then I heard a mechanical voice repeat over and over again:

A little robot quickly slid toward me and began to sniff at my fur. **SNIFF! SNIFF! SNIFF!**

"It's him!" the robot exclaimed. "It's Geronimo Stinton!"

Even though I was **SUSPENDED** in midair, I found the strength to correct the tiny machine.

"Excuse me, my name is Stilton, *Geronimo Stilton*!" I insisted.

Suddenly, the steel clamp on my tail released and I fell to the floor with a **thud**. I looked up just as a small door flew open. I instantly recognized a **familiar** snout.

"Professor von Volt!" I exclaimed. "What are you doing here?"

THE FORMULA FOR TIME TRAVEL

Professor von Volt and I have been friends for a long time. He's a **FASCINATING** mouse who has devoted his life to making new scientific **discoveries**. Unfortunately, I never know where to find him. That's because he has a habit of constantly moving his **SECRET** lab without telling anyone because he doesn't want other mice to know what he's working on! That means he usually has to **seek** me out when he needs my help with one of his projects or experiments.

PROFESSOR PAWS VON VOLT

"Geronimo!" he **EXCLAIMED**, giving me a

big hug. "What do you think of my new lab?"

I looked around the huge subterranean room. In front of me was a big steel desk covered in glass TEST TUBES and beakers. Each one was filled with a mysterious COLORED liquid. The test tubes bubbled and emitted a variety of stinky vapors. I also noticed several sheets of paper covered with sketches and scientific FORMULAS.

"Geronimo, I sent you that MYSTERIOUS letter because I wanted to be sure no one could figure out where my laboratory is," the professor explained. "But I wanted you to come here so that I could show you my latest and greatest invention!"

"A new invention?" I asked, intrigued.

"Yes!" the professor squeaked with excitement. "It's a machine that allows mice to TRAVEL THROUGH TIME!"

He pointed to a MYSTERIOUS object in the center of the room that was covered with a sheet.

3×3=?

Here it is . . . the time machine!

Professor von Volt's Notes

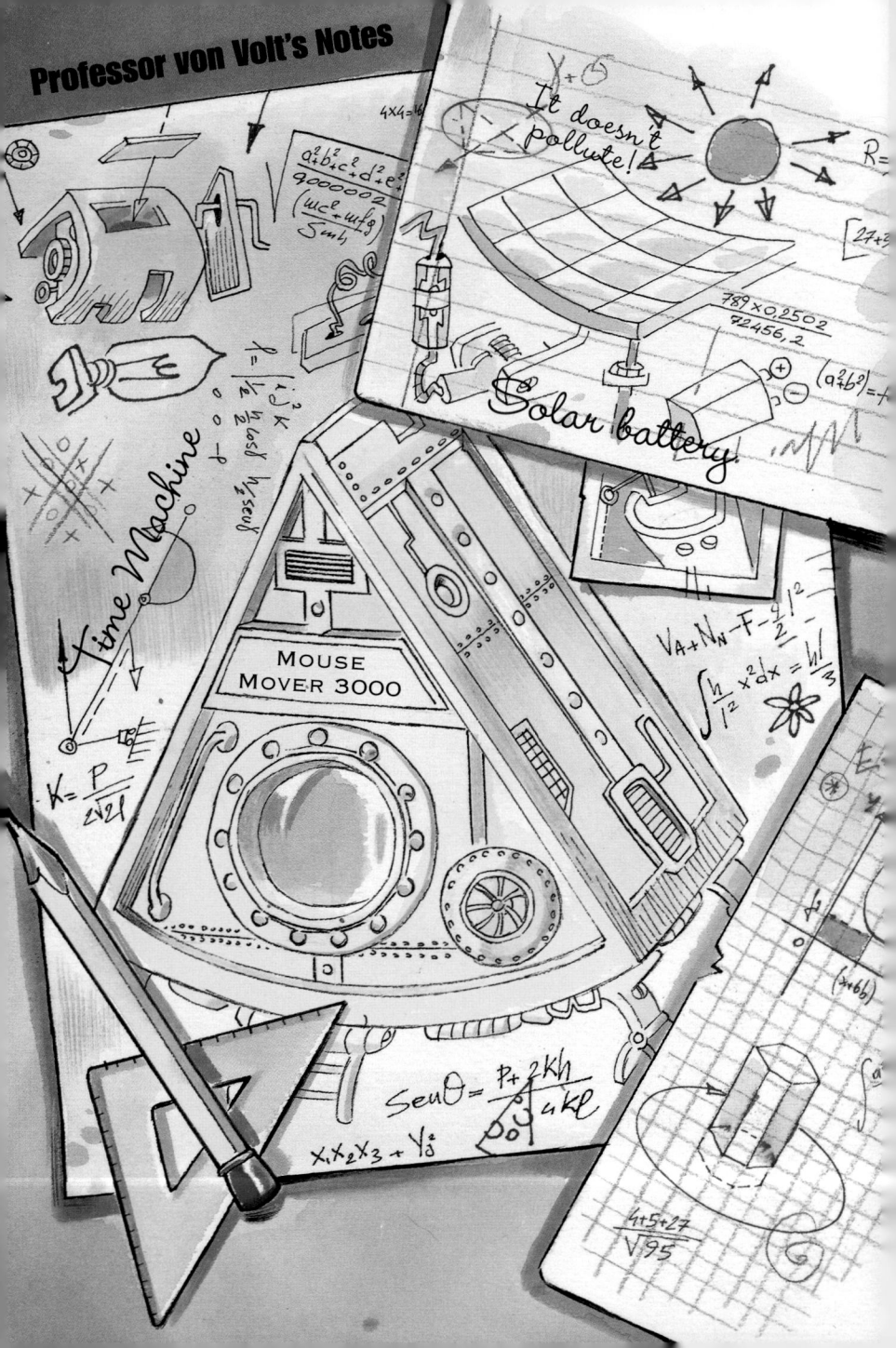

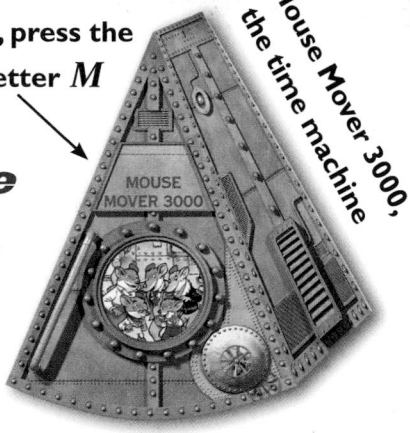

Mouse Mover 3000, the time machine

"You mean it's a ***time machine***?" I asked, amazed.

Professor von Volt lifted the sheet off the object to reveal a brass time machine shaped liked an **ENORMOUSE** slice of cheese. An engraving on it read: **MOUSE MOVER 3000**.

"This time machine can travel ***forward*** and **BACKWARD** in time," the professor explained. "It can also move in and out of **PARALLEL WORLDS** like a Möbius strip."

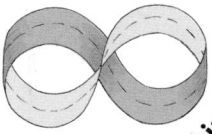

Möbius strip

I looked inside the time machine: It had a bright **BRASS** finish with solid bolts. I noticed five velvet-backed chairs that looked like dentist's chairs, except they were equipped with sturdy **SAFETY BELTS**.

Professor von Volt explained that to travel,

The Mysterious Möbius Strip

This fascinating play-experiment makes us think of the three dimensions and of the mystery of parallel worlds. The German mathematician and astronomer August Ferdinand Möbius (1790–1868) discovered the Möbius strip in 1858.

∞ is the shape of the Möbius strip and the symbol for infinity in mathematics.

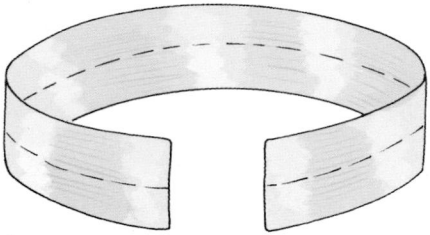

Take a strip of paper and color each side a different color.

Take a strip of paper . . .

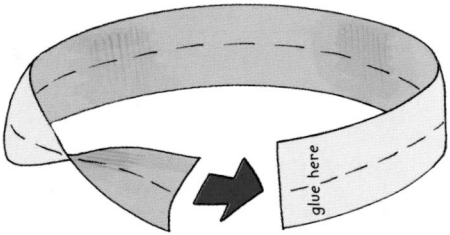

. . . twist it and glue it . . .

Twist the strip as shown and glue it as indicated. Is the purple side on the inside or the outside? How about the yellow side? Notice that the strip only has one side and one edge. If you trace your finger along the length of the strip, your finger will return to the starting point without crossing the edge of the strip.

. . . and cut it down the middle!

Now cut the strip down the middle. Surprise! The strip doesn't break into two pieces. Instead, it becomes an even longer strip with another twist in it.

one only had to program the CHRONOMETER, which was a super-advanced timepiece, with where and when to visit!

Right next to the Chronometer was a red button labeled PRESS HERE.

PROFESSOR VON VOLT continued to explain how the time machine worked.

"Geronimo, do you know about Albert Einstein's THEORY OF RELATIVITY?" he asked me.

"Well, I learned it in school, but . . ." My snout turned purple with embarrassment. I didn't

Albert Einstein (1879–1955)
Albert Einstein was a German physicist. His theory of relativity explained the important link between space and time using the formula $E=mc^2$. Einstein's work helped launch a new era in theoretical physics.

remember a **THING** about Einstein's theory!

"Well, in Einstein's formula $E=mc^2$, **energy** is equal to **MASS** times the **SPEED OF LIGHT** squared, right?" the professor asked.

"Yes, of course," I replied.

"One evening I decided to take a **warm** bath," Professor von Volt continued. "I grabbed a cube of **cheese** to snack on as I soaked. I **GNAWED** it quickly, and it disappeared in an instant. The cheese was transferred to another dimension — my **STOMACH**! Suddenly, I developed a new formula:

$$E=(mc)(vmg)^3$$

*Energy = the **mass** of the **cheese** times the **velocity** at which the **mouse gnawed** it, **cubed**!*

"When I did some calculations using my new formula, I discovered it was possible to travel through time!" the professor continued. "I'm leaving on my first journey as SOON as possible, and I need some passengers for the MOUSE MOVER 3000. Would you and your family like to come?"

The universe has three dimensions: height, width, and depth. Some consider time a fourth dimension and argue that time travel is possible!

"M-m-me?" I squeaked. "Oh, no, Professor, I couldn't."

Suddenly, Thea's and Trap's faces POPPED into my mind. I knew the two of them would love to go on a trip through time. I sighed. I couldn't say no.

"Professor, the Stilton family would be honored to travel with you!" I told him.

I'LL BE RIGHT THERE!

Geronimo Stilton

I called *The Rodent's Gazette*. My sister, Thea, answered the phone.

"Can you keep a **secret**?" I whispered. "Professor von Volt invented a ***time machine*** and invited us to travel with him. Get your things ready, and meet me as soon as you can!"

"Let me grab my **CAMERA**, and I'll be right there!" she shouted. "What a **FABUMOUSE** scoop!"

"Shhh!" I said. "Talk **softly**. Somebody might hear you!"

Thea Stilton

"I won't whisper a **SQUEAK** to anyone," Thea promised. "I give you my **rodent's word**! I'll pass you on to Trap."

A moment later, Trap got on the phone.

"What's this about a **TRIP** with the professor?" he shouted. "Look, I'll come only if there's going to be some decent **food**!"

"***Shhh!***" I said frantically. "Please don't **YELL**! It's a secret! A super-classified secret!"

"Okay, okay," he grumbled. "I'll come. But if there's a treasure involved, I want my share! **Rodent's word**, okay?"

"Yes, yes, yes," I agreed **HURRIEDLY**. "We'll talk about it later. In the meantime, get here on the double. We're about to **leave**."

"It's a deal!" Trap replied. "But first, I want to try out a new **joke** on you."

"Okay, okay," I agreed. "But ***HURRY***!"

"What did the mouse say when the **cat** bit his tail?" he asked.

"Hmmm . . . er . . . gee . . . well, it depends how **BIG** the cat is. . . ." I said.

"Gerry Berry, you have no sense of humor!" Trap groaned.

"Trap!" I complained. "You know I hate it when you call me that."

Trap handed the phone to my nephew Benjamin, who giggled.

"Uncle, the **MOUSE** said, '**That's the end of me!**'" he squeaked. "Get it?"

I **chuckled** at the joke.

"Is it **true**?" Benjamin asked once he stopped **laughing**.

"Are you really going to **TRAVEL** through time? Please, please take me along!"

"I'd **love** to take you, Benjamin," I explained, "but it could be a very **DANGEROUS** trip!"

"It won't be **DANGEROUS** if I'm with you, Uncle," Benjamin replied. "I know you'll protect me. Please take me, Uncle. **Pretty please?!**"

I sighed. I can never say no to Benjamin.

"Okay, my little morsel of **cheese**," I agreed with a smile. "You can come, too!"

"Thank you, Uncle!" he **squeaked**. "Thank you, thank you! You're the **best** uncle in the world!"

He handed the phone back to Thea, and I told her how to find Professor von Volt's **SECRET** laboratory.

Half an hour later, I heard the sound of the **GONG**.

Thea, Trap, and Benjamin had arrived!

I heard the sound of the gong. . . .
Bonggggg
Bonggggg
Bonggggg
Bonggggg

SAUSAGE FOR DINOSAURS

Professor von Volt opened a little refrigerator.

"I've been saving this bottle for years," he explained. "I've been waiting for a special occasion, and this is it!"

Trap examined the bottle with a knowing air.

"Phew," my cousin whistled. He was obviously

Photo taken by Thea

impressed. "This is a milkshake made of French Roquefort cheese from 1958. It's veeeerrry expensive! And I'll bet it's WHISKER-LICKING good. You have very good taste, Professor."

Thea took a group PHOTO as Benjamin shook the professor's paw.

"And now, let's go over a few SAFETY precautions," the professor told us.

1 "FIRST: The Chronometer must always be programmed with your desired destination. Be very careful! If you enter the wrong information, we could get lost in time!"

Holey cheese! I would be extremely careful. I didn't want to get lost in time!

The professor took something out of his pocket.

2 "SECOND: You'll need earplugs because the trip will be rather noisy."

He handed out the earplugs.

"By the way, does anyone get airsick?" he asked.

"Geronimo gets airsick, seasick, train sick, bus sick, and even taxi sick," Trap **SNICKERED**.

"Hmmm," the professor said. "Well, then, dear Geronimo, you'll probably experience a little nausea. But don't worry. Each trip takes exactly **Sixty Seconds** — no more, no less!

3 "**THIRD**: The past cannot be modified in any way, shape, or form, or it will change the future with disastrous consequences!

TRAVEL NECESSITIES:

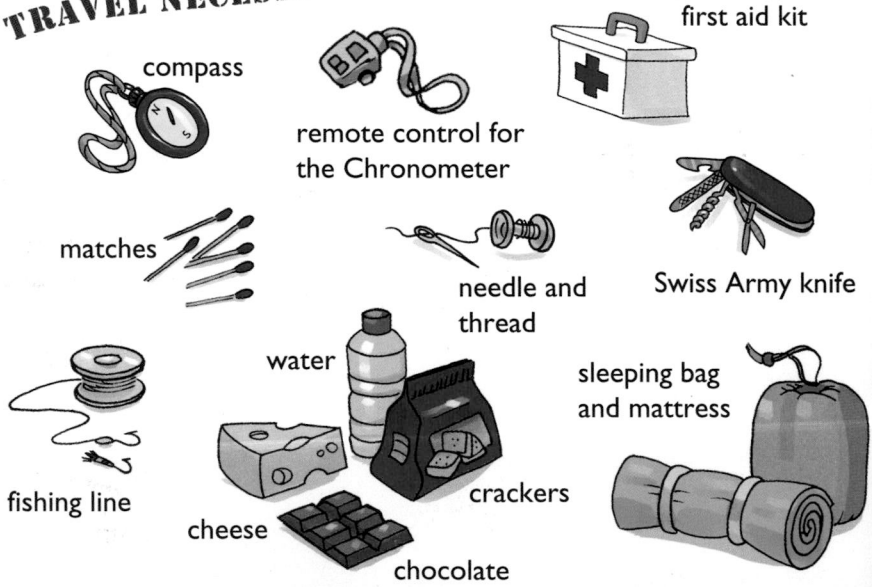

4 "**FOURTH**: Keep my *Time Travel Survival Manual* handy at all times."

He waved the manual at us.

"This could **SAVE** your life!" he shouted. "For example, if you encounter a dinosaur, check the manual to find out if it's an **HERBIVORE** or a **CARNIVORE**! If it's a carnivore, you'd better run as fast as you can!"

YIKES!

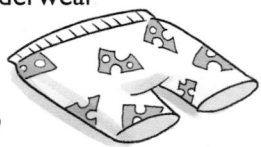

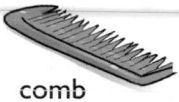

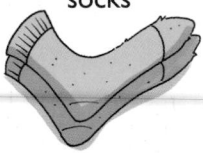

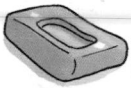

Then Professor von Volt became even more **SERIOUS**.

"Our secret journey through time has three **objectives**," he told us.

- In the **prehistoric period**: Find out why dinosaurs became extinct!

- In **ancient Egypt**: Find out how Cheops, the Great Pyramid of Giza, was built!

- In **medieval England**: Uncover the secrets of King Arthur and his court!

I had to remember everything about the **amazing** adventure I was about to take.

So I slipped a plastic envelope containing my **TRAVEL JOURNAL** and *pencil* into my pocket.

Meanwhile, Trap muttered, "What if we never make it back? We could become **sausage** for dinosaurs! Or a pharaoh might bury us alive in a giant **SARCOPHAGUS**! Or we might end up **skewered** like mouse kebabs on a medieval knight's sword!"

"Don't worry!" Benjamin piped up confidently. "Uncle Geronimo will **PROTECT** us."

He looked at me with such hope in his eyes. **Moldy mozzarella!** I really, really hoped I could live up to my dear nephew's expectations.

A Mysterious Blue Fog

I climbed into the ***time machine*** first. Trap, Thea, Benjamin, and the professor were still gathering their things.

"Would you please pass me the compass, the remote control for the **CHRONOMETER**, and the first aid kit?" I asked Trap.

"Sure thing, Cuz," Trap replied. Then he began

to **juggle** the three objects in the air.

I shook my head in **DISMAY**. Why, oh, why did my cousin have to be such a jokester?

Suddenly, Trap **TRIPPED** over one of the many stacks of books and papers Professor von Volt had around his lab.

The **COMPASS** went flying into the dashboard.

CRASH!

The **remote control** bonked me in the head.

CLONK!

And the **FIRST AID KIT** hit the door of the **MOUSE MOVER 3000**, causing it to slam shut.

THUD!

"**OUCHIE!**" I cried.

To my **horror**, I realized that the remote control had

activated the CHRONOMETER. I tried to jump out of the time machine, but the door was stuck. It was too late!

The MOUSE MOVER 3000 began spinning faster and faster.

I heard an extremely LOUD sound and understood why the professor had suggested earplugs. The little ship filled with a mysterious BLUE FOG, and I heard a huge bang.

BANGGGGGGGGGGGGGGG!

The time machine came to a sudden stop. Dazed, I gripped the armchair and waited for my head to stop spinning. It felt as if tiny butterflies were flying around it.

Worried, I called out to the others.

"Thea?" I shouted. "Trap? Benjamin? Professor

von Volt? Are you out there?"

No one answered.

Cautiously, I pressed the **BUttON** to open the door.

I raised my head and looked outside.

I was
left
breathless
with
amazement!

Journey through time . . .

Journey through time . . .

Journey through time . . .

Journey through time . . .

Journey through time . . .

Journey through time . . .

Journey through time . . .

Journey through time . . .

Journey through time . . .

Journey through time . . .
Journey through time . . .
Journey through time . . .

THE JURASSIC PERIOD
199 to 145 million years ago
Archaeopteryx
Ginkgo biloba leaf
Brachiosaurus
Ichthyosaurus
Ferns
Dryosaurus
Megazostrodon
Prehistoric mushrooms

Conifers
Rhamphorhynchus
Diplodocus
Stegosaurus
Cycads
Ceratosaurus

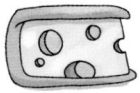

I Got Lost in Time!

It was such an awesome sight I had to pinch my tail to make sure I wasn't **DReaming**. I saw tall flowerless trees packed with **LUSH** leaves with strange cones instead of fruit. There were bushes of ferns and horsetails.

Between the leaves, I saw the neck of a **DIPLODOCUS** emerge from a **pond**. Next to it was the armored tail of a **STEGOSAURUS**. In the distance, a volcano shot a puff of vapor into the air, and the earth trembled.

PREHISTORY

DIPLODOCUS

Size: Up to ninety feet long
Found: North America
Distinguishing Characteristics: Its neck alone was as long as twenty-six feet! Diplodocus used its tail like a whip and traveled in herds.

A flying reptile silently glided by.

I glanced at the **CHRONOMETER**:

I was in the **Jurassic period**, the era of the **DINOSAURS**! I tried to reprogram the **CHRONOMETER**, but it was no use. It was stuck.

Holey cheese! What was I going to do? I was going to be **DINNER** for the

PREHISTORY

STEGOSAURUS

Size: Up to thirty feet long
Found: North America
Distinguishing Characteristics: Herbivorous dinosaur that lived during the late Jurassic period. The bony plates on its back and tail arose from its skin, not its skeleton.

dinos! It was just as I had feared. I, Geronimo Stilton, was lost in time!

I shut myself inside the time machine and began to sob.

"I'm alone and far away from home!" I sobbed. "I'm scared! I'm extremely scared! I'm ridiculously scared out of my mind!"

Suddenly, I remembered the nursery rhyme my **aunt Sweetfur** always sang to me when I was a little MOUSELING who was afraid of the dark.

If your courage fails you,
Do not be afraid. . . .
Eat a little cheese
And do not be dismayed.
Little mouse, you'll be okay
If you know what to do. . . .
Be brave and calm and carry on,
And you will make it through!

I sighed. At that point, Aunt Sweetfur would always give me a little kiss and offer me a **morsel** of cheese.

I would ask her, "Auntie, does cheese make **FEAR** go away?"

She always had the same answer.

"No, little one," she'd say with a sweet smile. "But it tastes ***delicious***!"

I sighed. Oh, Aunt Sweetfur!

All mouselings deserve a special aunt like her!

To give myself a little **courage**, I began talking to myself in a loud voice.

"Everything's fine," I shouted. "I'm going to make it!"

I repeated it **over** and **over** again.

"Of course I'm going to make it! I will make it. I will make it. I will make it!"

I picked myself up, stood up straight, and opened the porthole. Then I climbed out of the ship, took a deep breath, and entered the **prehistoric** forest.

It was humid outside and very, very **hot**. I took out my travel journal and made some notes:

I find myself in a humid forest during the Jurassic period. I am alone, alone, alone, and it is extremely hot!

Oh, why, oh, why did the **Jurassic** period have to be so hot? I was **ROASTING** like a mouse **KEBAB**! Suddenly, it became shady

and cool. I breathed a sigh of relief.

"Ah, how **wonderful**!" I exclaimed. "The sky is getting cloudy, and I'll have a break from this terrible heat. . . ."

I looked up to the sky, but I had barely lifted my head when an **ENORMOUSE** Rhamphorhynchus grabbed me in its claws and **MOUSENAPPED** me!

I Don't Want to Be a Dino Snack!

"**Heeeelp!**" I squeaked. "I want to get off!"

But the Rhamphorhynchus kept on **FLYING**.

"**Holey cheese!**" I cried as the wind rushed through my fur. "This breeze is really cooling me off!"

Ophthalmosaurus

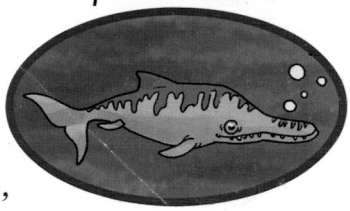

We **hovered** over a lake. Here and there among the waves swam Ophthalmosaurus, **marine** reptiles that are similar to dolphins. On the **LAKESHORE**, I saw a herd of Protosuchus, which are similar to **CROCODILES**. As we flew over, the Protosuchus raised their snouts and opened their jaws. **snap! snap!**

"Let me **goooooooooo**!" I shouted to the Rhamphorhynchus.

But the beast didn't listen. Then I had an idea: I reached up and **TICKLED** its belly! The creature dropped me immediately. I ***PLUMMETED*** down and landed on something soft.

"Ah!" I exclaimed as I massaged my sore tail. "I'm finally free!"

Then I turned to see two enormouse yellow **EYES** staring at me. ***SQUEEEEEEAK!*** It

was an **Allosaurus**!

I tried to think. Was Allosaurus **HERBIVOROUS** or **carnivorous**? **HERBIVOROUS** or **carnivorous**? **HERBIVOROUS** or **carnivorous**?

He opened his mouth wide, and I saw his jaws bristling with **RAZOR-SHARP** teeth.

"Allosaurus is **carnivoroooous**!" I yelled. "I don't want to become a dinosaur's snack! **HEEEEEEEELP!**"

I ran through the forest as ***FAST*** as I could.

I ran and ran and ran. Suddenly, I found myself

in front of a **SLAB** of rock. I was **trapped**! The Allosaurus came closer, **studying** me with mean, beady eyes. He looked **hungry**. **VERRRRY** hungry.

The **Allosaurus** took a step closer. My whiskers quivered in fear. Then I heard another **ROAR**.

PREHISTORY

ALLOSAURUS

Size: Up to forty-five feet long
Found: North America, Africa, and Australia
Distinguishing Characteristics: Allosaurus was the largest carnivorous dinosaur in the Jurassic period. Its name means "different reptile." It had more than seventy long, sharp serrated teeth and slashing claws on its small arms. It also had bony knobs and ridges on the top of its head.

. . . a dinosaur's snack!

PREHISTORY

MEGALOSAURUS

Size: Up to thirty feet long
Found: Europe
Distinguishing Characteristics: Megalosaurus was a carnivorous dinosaur that lived during the Jurassic period. Its name means "great lizard." Its front claws had three fingers with slashing claws, which were designed for gripping prey.

"Roaaaaaaar!"

It was a **hungry-looking Megalosaurus**! Chewy cheddar **cheese sticks** — didn't these dinosaurs ever have a **SQUARE** meal? Then maybe they wouldn't be so interested in a tiny mouse snack like me!

I **CRAWLED** behind a tree trunk and tried to make myself very, very small.

What could be worse than one hungry dinosaur? I thought to myself. The answer: **TWO** hungry dinosaurs!

"Urgghhhhhhh . . ." said the Allosaurus.

"Kkreeoookkkkkkkk!" replied the Megalosaurus.

"Gnkkkkgrrkkkkkkkkkk!" roared the Allosaurus.

I didn't stick around to hear what the Megalosaurus had to say in reply. Instead, I ran breathlessly toward the **MOUSE MOVER 3000** and jumped inside. I closed the porthole with a slam.

The two beasts **POUNDED** on the ship, trying to get me to come out.

"Krrrrrkkkkttgnkkkkk!"

Suddenly, the **CHRONOMETER** started to buzz. Holey cheese! It had come unstuck! I was going to **escape** the Jurassic period . . . but where was I going now? I was about to find out.

BANG!

I'LL NEVER, EVER, EVER GET HOME AGAIN!

After several hums and buzzes, the **MOUSE MOVER 3000** stopped. The **CHRONOMETER** read:

I peeked out the porthole. I was still in **prehistoric** times, but the scenery had changed. I was in the **Cretaceous period**!

First I had been mousenapped by a flying reptile, and then I almost became an Allosaurus's

CRETACEOUS PERIOD
144 to 65 million years ago
Pteranodon
Palms
Torosaurus
Saurolophus
Archelon
Dromaeosaurus
Frog
Opossum
Snail
Salamander

Magnolia
Albertosaurus
Ouranosaurus
Heron ancestor
Equisetum
Panoplosaurus
Crocodile
Snake

snack. Could anything else possibly go wrong?

Uh-oh. Thinking of how I had almost become a dino **snack** made me realize how hungry I was. My tummy grumbled and rumbled, and I would have given anything for a tiny little **morsel** of cheese.

Did they even have **cheese** during the Cretaceous period? There was only one way to find out.

I climbed out of the **MOUSE MOVER 3000** and began to search around outside for something to eat. Suddenly, I heard a **rustle** behind me. I turned just in time to see the **MOUSE MOVER 3000** spinning around and around.

An instant later, the time machine had **VANISHED**!

"Oh, no!" I sobbed. "Now I'll **NEVER, EVER, EVER** get home again!"

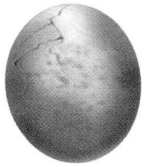

I'M NOT YOUR MOTHER!

Just when I thought things couldn't get any worse, it started to RAIN. I took cover under a ginkgo biloba leaf and curled up inside a large abandoned nest.

I cried as I thought of my family. Would I ever hug THEA and TRAP again? And I missed Benjamin so much! But crying wasn't going

to get me anywhere. So I opened the professor's *Time Travel Survival Manual* and began to read by the SILVERY light of the moon. The hours flew by. At dawn, I closed the book, satisfied. I now knew everything there was to know about PREHISTORIC TIMES!

Suddenly I heard a sound.

Tap, tap, tap!

I rummaged through the nest's leaves and found a large, delicate ivory-colored EGG.

The egg had a little CRACK in it. Suddenly, the crack began getting bigger and bigger. An odd-looking little head with two tiny surprised EYES popped out.

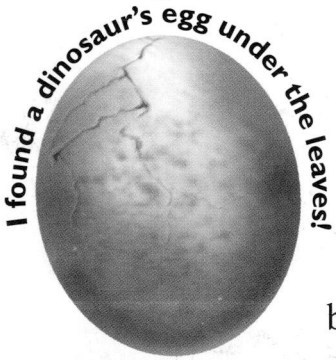

The eyes looked at me in AMAZEMENT.

It was a baby Triceratops!

"Snnniiiiiiiiiiiick!" the baby dinosaur howled.

I **STOOD** up. The baby dinosaur **STOOD** up!

I **scratched** my head. He **scratched** his head!

I **JUMPED** to the left. He **JUMPED** to the left!

I **JUMPED** to the right. He **JUMPED** to the right!

Why was he imitating me? **Why? Why? Why?**

Suddenly, I **UNDERSTOOD**: The baby Triceratops thought I was his **MOTHER** because I was the first living thing he saw when he came out of his egg!

"I'm not your mother," I told him. "I'm a **MOUSE**!"

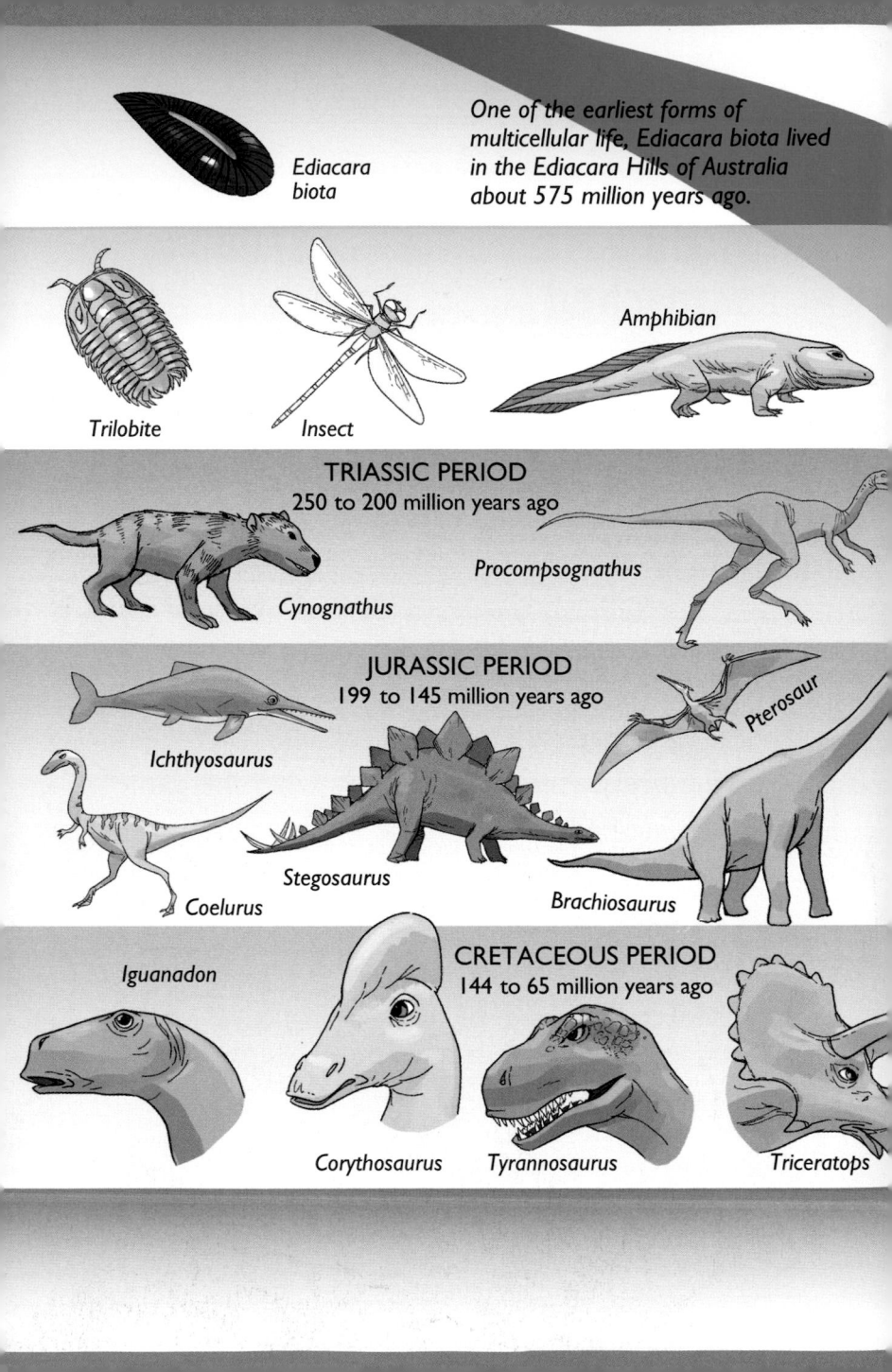
Ediacara biota
One of the earliest forms of multicellular life, Ediacara biota lived in the Ediacara Hills of Australia about 575 million years ago.
Trilobite
Insect
Amphibian
TRIASSIC PERIOD
250 to 200 million years ago
Cynognathus
Procompsognathus
JURASSIC PERIOD
199 to 145 million years ago
Ichthyosaurus
Pterosaur
Coelurus
Stegosaurus
Brachiosaurus
CRETACEOUS PERIOD
144 to 65 million years ago
Iguanadon
Corythosaurus
Tyrannosaurus
Triceratops

PROTEROZOIC EON
2.5 billion to 542 million years ago

PALEOZOIC ERA
542 to 251 million years ago

Scientists subdivide the history of Earth into ERAS and PERIODS. Dinosaurs developed during the MESOZOIC ERA, which is divided into three periods: the TRIASSIC, JURASSIC, and CRETACEOUS.

MESOZOIC ERA
250 to 65 million years ago

Dinosaurs appeared around 230 million years ago and disappeared around 65 million years ago.

Anchisaurus

CENOZOIC ERA
65 million years ago to today

The carnivorous dino with the biggest teeth: They were a foot long!

Tyrannosaurus rex

Compsognathus

The smallest dinosaur: It was the size of a turkey!

The most armored dinosaur: It had a bony-plated back!

Stegosaurus

The loudest dinosaur: Its head had a bony megaphone!

Parasaurolophus

Triceratops

The oddest dinosaur: It had horns on its nose and forehead!

Diplodocus

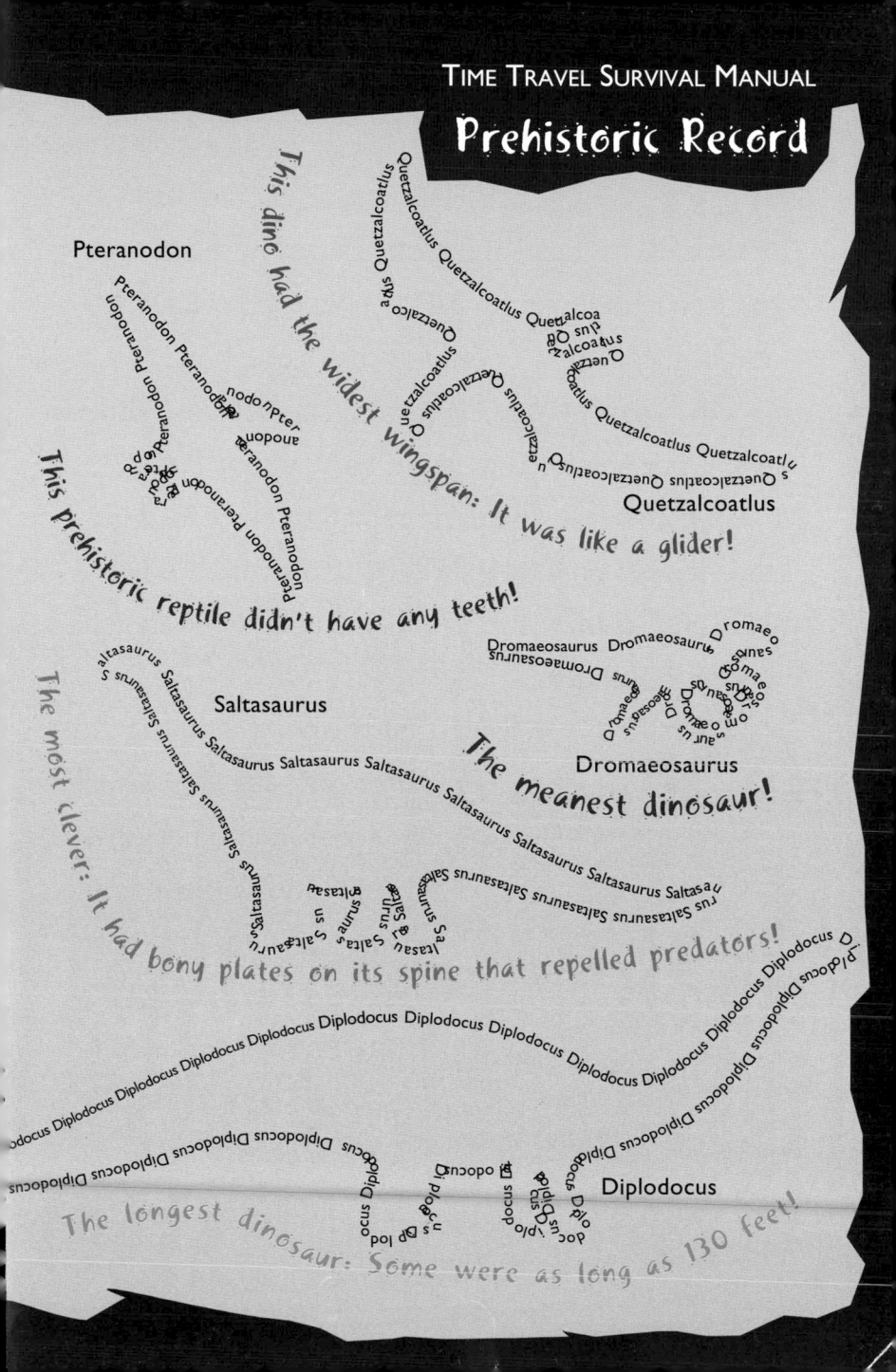
TIME TRAVEL SURVIVAL MANUAL
Prehistoric Record
Pteranodon
This dino had the widest wingspan: It was like a glider!
Quetzalcoatlus
This prehistoric reptile didn't have any teeth!
Saltasaurus
The meanest dinosaur!
Dromaeosaurus
The most clever: It had bony plates on its spine that repelled predators!
Diplodocus
The longest dinosaur: Some were as long as 130 feet!

He **tilted** his head and looked up at me as though he didn't understand. His eyes were so **sweet** and innocent that I couldn't just leave him.

"Oh, okay," I said. "I'll take care of you, little guy. First, you need a name. How about **TOPS**?"

Tops nodded. The early morning air was chilly, and Tops was **shivering** from the cold. So I covered him with my jacket, and he soon fell asleep in the nest.

I leaned back and was about to doze off myself when someone pinched my tail and shrieked in my ear: "**HERBIVOROUS** or **carnivorous**? **HERBIVOROUS** or **carnivorous**? **HERBIVOROUS** or **carnivorous**?"

PREHISTORY

TRICERATOPS

Size: Up to twenty-nine feet long
Found: North America
Distinguishing Characteristics: This herbivorous dinosaur lived during the end of the Cretaceous period. Its name means "three-horned face" because of its large horns and bony frill. Triceratops lived in herds.

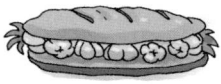

TRICERATOPS STEW?

"If I'd been carnivorous, you'd be **DEAD** by now!" my cousin Trap said with a chuckle.

I couldn't believe it! I'd never been so glad to see my cousin. And he wasn't **alone** — Professor von Volt, Thea, and Benjamin were there, too!

"I'm so **happy** to see all of you!" I exclaimed.

Professor von Volt explained that he was able to recall the **MOUSE MOVER 3000** with a special **EMERGENCY** telecommand.

I told him all about my adventures in the Jurassic period.

Benjamin and Tops became instant **FRIENDS**.

But Trap eyed the adorable dinosaur with HUNGRY eyes.

"I know what we're having for dinner tonight," Trap announced. "We'll have Triceratops stew. Yummy!"

"Don't even think about it!" I scolded Trap. "He's my friend. We can make a vegetable soup instead."

I looked at the plant life around me, and I recognized some modern plants, like oak, magnolias, papyrus, and water lilies. Surely we could find at least a few that were EDIBLE.

Suddenly, Trap got a mischievous glint in his eye.

"Okay, Cuz," he said. "Veggie stew it is. You just leave everything up to me."

I Could Have Become Extinct!

While Trap worked on dinner, Thea, the professor, and I built a little **WOODEN** hut on top of a tree branch to protect us from **prehistoric** snakes and insects.

A few hours later, Trap called me over. He lifted the lid on a pot of soup that was bubbling over the fire. It smelled **DELICIOUS**!

"Taste it," Trap urged me. "Tell me **truthfully** what you think. I trust you!"

FLATTERED, I tasted a spoonful of soup.

"So?" Trap asked. "Do you like it?"

"It's good."

He stared at me.

"You feel fine?"

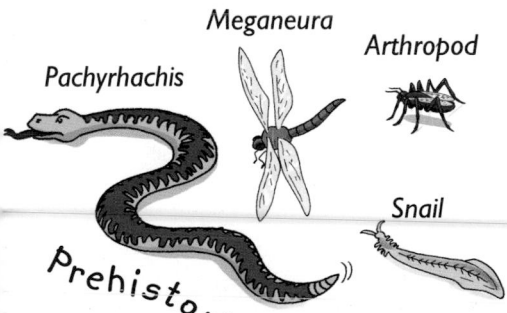

Prehistoric snakes and insects

"Of course! Why wouldn't I?"

"Really? **Fine?**"

"Yes," I said, beginning to get impatient. "I feel totally fine! **Why wouldn't I?**"

"Okay, soup's on!" Trap yelled. "**LET'S EAT!**"

"What's in the soup?" I asked distractedly.

"Some little prehistoric **MUSHROOMS**!" Trap replied proudly.

"**Prehistoric mushrooms?**" Thea asked **SUSPICIOUSLY**, her spoon in midair. "How do you know they're not **POISONOUS**?"

"Simple!" Trap replied.

"I had Geronimo **taste** them. I'm a very careful mouse!"

"You tested them on me?" I squeaked. "I could have been **poisoned**! I could have gone extinct!"

"Well, what was I supposed to put in the pot?" Trap whined. "You wouldn't let me **EAT** the Triceratops, so . . ."

"Gentlemice," Professor von Volt said with a smile. "Let's not argue. I have a special treat."

Then he opened a small box and showed us five slices of aged **Gouda**.

We each took a piece of cheese.

"Let's celebrate that our dear Geronimo is with us again," said the professor.

"To Geronimo!" Thea agreed, **RAISING** her slice of cheese.

"To friendship!" I replied, raising my own slice. "I'm so glad we're together again."

Wooden box holding Professor Paws von Volt's collection of vintage cheeses

THE DINOSAURS' SECRET

The following morning we got up at **dawn** and had breakfast.

Trap made us tea using the leaves of a prehistoric plant, and **scrambled** prehistoric bird eggs spiced with a wild root that tasted like onion.

While we ate, Professor von Volt explained our **mission** to us.

"Dear friends," he began. "We don't know whether the dinosaurs became **extinct** slowly over time or whether it happened more rapidly. But more important, we don't know **WHY** it happened. We're here now to gather the data to help us **UNDERSTAND**. Here are the various hypotheses. . . ."

WHY DID
DINOSAURS
BECOME
EXTINCT?

HYPOTHESIS NUMBER 1

Some scientists believe a gigantic meteorite hit the Earth at the end of the Cretaceous period. The cloud of dust that was raised by its impact prevented the rays of the sun from reaching plant and animal life on Earth. As a result, the climate became colder, and many plants and animals died off and became extinct.

The evidence that supports this hypothesis includes the fact that a high quantity of iridium, which is rare on Earth but common in meteorites, was discovered in rocks that date back to the end of the Cretaceous period. Furthermore, a crater 124 miles long and more than 2,500 feet deep was discovered in the Gulf of Mexico, and scientists believe the crater was formed by the impact of an ancient meteorite.

HYPOTHESIS NUMBER 2

Some scientists believe a climatic change at the end of the Cretaceous period — perhaps one caused by a gigantic volcanic eruption — covered the Earth with lava and smoke. The cloud of ash from the eruption prevented the rays of the sun from reaching plant and animal life on Earth. Some animals were able to adapt to the new climate, but unfortunately, the dinosaurs were not among them.

HYPOTHESIS NUMBER 3

At the end of the Cretaceous period, mammals began to thrive. Some scientists believe these mammals competed with dinosaurs for food and also fed on dinosaur eggs, which may have helped bring on the dinosaurs' extinction!

GOOD-BYE, FRIEND

I took a walk by the river and thought about Professor von Volt's theories. I took a breath of clean, fresh prehistoric air and felt truly grateful. I had been reunited with my family and was no longer lost in time! I felt so peaceful!

I returned to my friends, where we saw a herd of Triceratops drinking in the river.

"When you get BIG, you'll look like them," I told Tops. "You're a Triceratops, not a mouse. Be BRAVE and go join them!"

He hid shyly behind me and shook his head. I gently pushed him toward the group of Triceratops. Tentatively, he approached the herd. Each dinosaur sniffed little Tops, and then they made room for him. They had accepted him!

"Good-bye, little friend!" I called out as the herd walked away. "I will never FORGET you!"

A Living, Breathing Hang Glider!

We worked hard the entire day to collect as much **information** about the dinosaurs as we could.

At the end of the day, we stopped to rest in a forest of **EUCALYPTUS TREES**. While the others were putting up camp, I took a pail and went to the creek to get some **water**. Suddenly, I heard a terrible screech.

Eucalyptus leaf

"Grrraaauuukkkkk!"

It was a **HUGE** flying reptile. It had an enormouse sharp, pointed beak, and each wing was more than ten feet wide! It looked like a living, breathing **hang glider**!

"It's the largest prehistoric flying reptile!" Professor von Volt WHISPERED from behind me.

PREHISTORY

QUETZALCOATLUS

Size: Up to a fifty-foot wingspan
Found: North America
Distinguishing Characteristics: These flying reptiles lived during the Cretaceous period and ate fish. They could not take off from a level place because they were too heavy. Instead, they would launch from a slope and take advantage of the warm winds to carry them gliding through the air.

"QUETZALCOATLUS!"

He pointed to the creature's claw, which was caught in a thorny bush.

"Chances are it won't be able to free itself!" the professor said.

The reptile cried out again in **pain**, **fear**, and **ANGER**.

"Poor thing!" I murmured. "I'll help you!"

"Be careful, Geronimo," the professor warned me. "A wounded animal is always **dangerous**!"

I slowly reached over to cut the **THORNY** branches with a knife. A moment later, the creature's paw was freed. He stared at me for a few seconds. Then he climbed to the top of a eucalyptus tree and launched into the air.

HERE, DINO, DINO, DINO!

We packed up our camp and continued our **journey** the next day. I noticed something was following us in the air: It was the **Quetzalcoatlus** I had saved! I waved at it, and the reptile replied by **dipping** his head as if to say thank you before he flew away. It was an **INCREDIBLE** moment.

Then just a second later, I stubbed my toe on a fossil.

"**YEOW!**" I shouted. So much for my incredible moment!

I reached down to pick up an **AMAZING** fossilized fern leaf.

Fossils are the preserved remains of plants or animals that lived millions of years ago. Fossils are useful to scientists because they help them reconstruct prehistoric environments.

Fern leaf

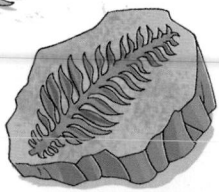

Fern fossil

"LOOK!" I showed Benjamin. "It's a fern fossil."

"Wow!" Benjamin exclaimed, looking up at me admiringly. "That's so cool, Uncle G."

"Well, Benjamin," Trap broke in, "if you think that's **cool**, look at this!"

Trap pointed to a small dinosaur with BRIGHTLY COLORED, scaly skin. It had long, sharp claws, and looked mean. As soon as the dinosaur saw Trap, a SECOND dinosaur sprung up behind it, and then a THIRD dinosaur emerged from a clump of ferns. Soon, a FOURTH, FIFTH, SIXTH, SEVENTH, and EIGHTH dinosaur appeared! Holey cheese — there were a lot of them!

"Here, dino, dino, dino," Trap cooed to the FIRST dinosaur.

"Uh, Trap," I warned, "I wouldn't do that. I'm getting a **BAD** feeling here. A very, very, very bad feeling!"

I quickly grabbed the *Time Travel Survival Manual* and frantically leafed through it. **HORRIFIED**, I began to read aloud:

"'The **Dromaeosaurus** is a small **carnivorous** dinosaur that hunts in packs.'"

Trap shrugged.

"So what?" he asked. "Come on, these little guys are as **sweet** as puppies. Isn't that right?"

Trap cooed at the dinosaurs again.

"Trap, I **REALLY** wouldn't —" I began, but Trap cut me off.

"You're such a **scaredy-mouse**, Geronimo!" Trap scoffed. "Let me show you. Here, dino, dino, dino. Come to Uncle Trap!"

He stretched out his arm and offered the little dinosaur a mushroom.

The dinosaur sniffed at the mushroom but then decided he would rather try a **bite** of Trap's

tasty-looking finger.

"YEOOOOW!" Trap cried.

I grabbed a bone and **waved** it in the air.

"Go away!" I shouted at the little Dromaeosaurus.

"Come any closer, and I'll

make dinosaur **MEATBALLS** out of you!" Trap added, waving a bone he had found as well.

But the dinosaur seemed to like the **taste** it had gotten of Trap's finger.

Suddenly, the pack **ATTACKED** all at once. They threw Trap on the ground, and one of them grabbed his arm with its sharp fangs. Who knows what would have happened if I hadn't **FURIOUSLY** waved the bone and shouted at the top of my lungs.

"**GO AWAYYYYYYYYYYYY!**" I yelled. "Scram!"

Taken by surprise, the Dromaeosaurs retreated and **SWIFTLY** took flight.

Poor Trap was as **pale** as a slice of mozzarella. I would have been, too, if the Dromaeosaurus had grabbed my arm.

"G-Geronimo . . ." Trap mumbled.

"What?" I asked.

He pointed to something **behind** me.

"G-Geronimo . . . the Ty-ty-ty . . ."

"What is it, Trap?" I urged him **bravely**. "Don't worry, I'll protect you!"

"Behind you!" he shrieked. "Turn around!"

I turned and found myself face-to-face with a

TYRANNOSAURUS REX!

PREHISTORY

TYRANNOSAURUS REX
Size: Up to forty feet long and thirteen feet tall
Found: North America
Distinguishing Characteristics: This carnivorous dinosaur lived at the end of the Cretaceous period. Its name means "tyrant lizard." It had a gigantic skull, short two-fingered arms, strong jaws, and long, sharp serrated teeth.

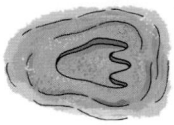

I'M AFRAID OF HEIGHTS!

Benjamin, smart little mouse that he is, had **climbed** to the top of a eucalyptus tree when the Dromaeosaurs attacked.

"Uncle Geronimo!" he shouted from the tree. "The Tyrannosaurus rex is **carnivorous**. Ruuuun!"

I **RAN** and **RAN** until I was out of breath. The T. rex's huge footsteps echoed through the forest, and the ground shook under its weight!

The T. rex was huge. I wasn't going to win this battle unless I used my wits! Then I had an idea. Right in front of me was a **deep** gorge with a **narrow** rock bridge over it. The bridge would hold my weight, but it would **collapse** under the weight of the T. rex! I scampered across, trying not to look down. **I'm afraid of heights!**

Squeak!
Boom!
Boom!

Once I got to the other side, the rock began to **crumble**, and the T. rex fell with a growl. But now how was I going to get back to the other side? Then I heard the **rustling** of wings. It was the Quetzalcoatlus!

"Please help me!" I **BEGGED**.

A second later, he allowed me to climb up onto his wings. Then he **gently** carried me back to my friends. Touched, I gave him a **BIG** hug.

This is the **secret** to real friendship: Support each other and try to always be there when a **friend** is in need!

THE VOICE OF THE PREHISTORIC FOREST

By the time I was reunited with my friends, **night** had fallen. The professor was tending to Trap's wounds. Meanwhile, Thea, who is an expert in survival techniques, rubbed two pieces of flint together. She used the **SPARK** to ignite some dried leaves. Then she slowly added pieces of bark, twigs, and large logs until we had a **BRIGHT**, burning fire.

She found five branches shaped like **FORKS** and carved five pieces of wood into **spoons** for all of us. Then she served up some

soup she had made in a carved-out gourd!

I offered to take my turn as the night watch. When everyone finally fell asleep, I realized I was the only one awake in the **dark**! The light from the fire threw eerie **shadows** on the cave walls. Outside the cave, I heard the voices of the forest — strange calls, growls, and funny cries echoed in the night.

How terrifying! Would we survive in the **wild** forest of the Cretaceous period? I **shivered** and held on to the Giganotosaurus bone I had used to fend off the herd of Dromaeosaurs.

I was sure of one thing: I would do anything to save my fur!

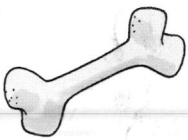

A Prehistoric Menu

Another day went by. Under Professor von Volt's direction, we picked up rock samples, took photos of plants and animals, and jotted down **INVALUABLE** notes.

"How come we haven't seen a **MAMMOTH** yet?" Trap asked.

"Mammoths appeared much later in history!" the professor explained. "And now I have an

Evolution of life:

One of the first multicellular beings

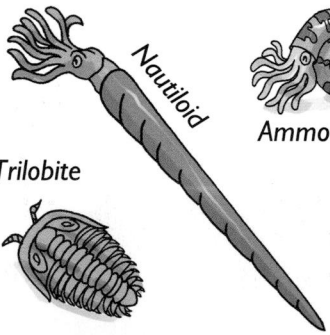

Ammonite

Dipnoi (lungfish)

Trilobite

Edaphosaurus

ANNOUNCEMENT. We've collected enough information to complete our mission in prehistoric times. If everyone agrees, we can leave **tomorrow**. Let's have a show of paws. . . ."

We all raised our **paws** at the same time.

Then Trap cleared his throat.

"I have an **announcement** as well," he said. "To celebrate the **greatest cook in the world** — by which I mean me — I'd like to prepare a **SPECIAL PREHISTORIC MENU** for you all tonight," Trap told us.

"Now, let's see . . . I brought all the **cheeses** from home, but I'll need help getting all the other supplies," Trap said.

He handed me a **LOOOOOOOOOOOOONG** list of ingredients to find.

"Here's what I need, Cuz," he said, giving me a little shove. "Hop to it!"

Holey cheese . . . there were some **strange** things on that list! Snails, breadfruit, algae, mollusks, sturgeon, hearts of palm, and figs. Where, oh, where was I going to find all this **STUFF**?

Luckily, Professor von Volt offered to **HELP** me.

"Don't worry, Geronimo," he told me. "I know exactly where we can get everything. **LET'S GO!**"

A Lake, a Sunset, and Two True Friends

Professor von Volt and I headed for the lake. As we walked, he pointed out all sorts of **AMAZING** specimens of plant and animal life to me. It was **incredible**!

When we got to the lake, the professor pulled a **NET** out of his backpack. Then he showed me how to scoop and strain algae. While I **harvested** the algae, he began hunting for **snails**.

BLECH!

That algae was so slippery and **slimy**, and it smelled awful! In fact, it had the most **TERRIBLE** stench! I really hoped Trap's **WORLD-FAMOUSE** recipe would make it taste better than it smelled.

PREHISTORY

SALTASAURUS

Size: Up to thirty-nine feet long
Found: South America
Distinguishing Characteristics: This herbivorous dinosaur lived at the end of the Cretaceous period. Its body was armored with bony plates that were embedded in its skin.

As I scooped the algae, I suddenly noticed a dinosaur with a very

LOOOOOOOOOONG neck just a few feet away from me. It was a **Saltasaurus**!

I immediately knew it was herbivorous because it was happily munching on the juiciest buds on a very **TALL** poplar tree.

"Splendid, isn't it?" Professor von Volt asked.

"**Nature** is life's greatest treasure!"

I nodded in agreement, **AWESTRUCK** by the sight of the enormouse dinosaur right in front of me.

"Dearest Geronimo, there's something that's been weighing on me," the professor continued.

"I've been thinking about **extinction**.

"Whenever a species dies out, it's **TRAGIC**," Professor von Volt explained. "Many species — like the **DINOSAURS** — became extinct during prehistoric times. But even today, animals like tigers, whales, and pandas are at **RISK**. The destruction of these animals' natural habitats, hunting, and pollution all contribute to the problem."

He shook his head **SADLY**.

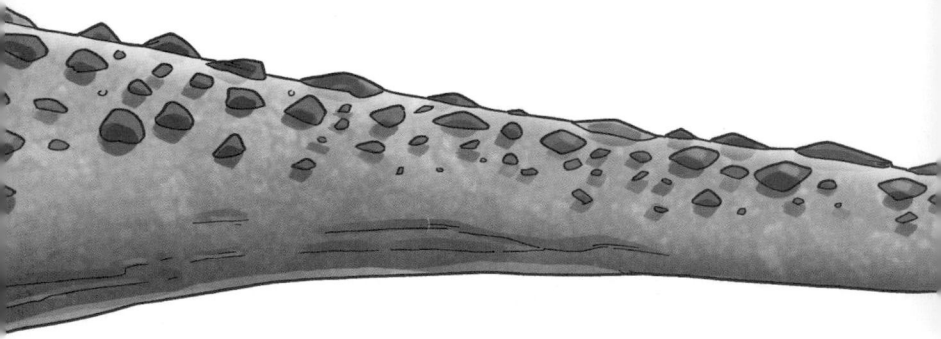

"The natural equilibrium of nature needs to be *respected*!" Professor von Volt continued. "Nature is WISER than we think."

We sat along the bank of the small lake, dangling our paws in the water.

A prehistoric lake, a PINK sunset, and true friendship.

What more could a mouse ask for in life?

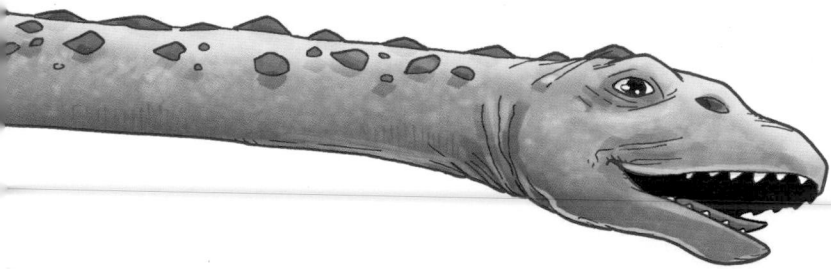

THE GREATEST COOK IN THE WORLD

Professor von Volt and I brought Trap the **ingredients** we had gathered. He stood at the fire and sang while he worked:

crunch crunch crunch crunch crunch crunch

A true cook doesn't need pots and pans,

He'll make do with whatever he can!

A real cook can serve any number of mice,

He can whip up a feast from nothing but rice!

He doesn't need help from any of you,

To make the world's most excellent stew!

crunch crunch crunch crunch crunch crunch

A tiny Compsognathus came nosing around trying to **STEAL** some of Trap's food. At first,

Trap **SHOOED** the **DINOSAUR** away, but then he **SOFTENED** and threw him a little morsel.

PREHISTORY

COMPSOGNATHUS

Size: About three feet long
Found: Europe
Distinguishing Characteristics: This tiny carnivorous dinosaur lived at the end of the Jurassic period. Its name means "graceful jaw." It was one of the smallest dinosaurs, and it fed on worms and small lizards.

"Here's a little meat," Trap whispered. "You should have a good meal tonight, too!"

Trap was true to his word — our dinner was **delicious**! We went to sleep feeling full and **HAPPY**.

But at five in the morning, the earth began to

RAIN OF HOT RED STONES

I woke up with a start and saw hundreds of meteorites **streaking** across the sky.

"**METEORITES!**" Professor von Volt shouted. "The dinosaurs might be about to go extinct!"

There was **CHAOS** all around us. Herds of **terrorized** dinosaurs galloped through the forest, knocking down shrubs and trees as they fled.

"It's time for us to go to **Egypt** to find out how Cheops — that is, the Great Pyramid of Giza — was built!"

With trembling paws, the professor programmed the Chronometer.

A meteorite CRASHED to Earth right next to us! The ground beneath my paws trembled forebodingly.

Suddenly, a thick, smelly, and slimy black substance rained down on me from above. I looked up to see the tail of a huge dinosaur going by.

"Dinosaur dung!" I squeaked. I tried to wipe it off, but instead I slipped and landed in an even BIGGER heap of it! I tried desperately to extract myself, but it was useless. I was stuck!

"Don't worry, Uncle!" Benjamin called.

"We'll pull you out, little brother!" Thea shouted.

Then Thea, Benjamin, and Trap grabbed my tail and pulled me out. Plop!

To wash me off, my cousin threw a bucket of freezing water on my face. SPLASH!

"I want to go **HOOOOOOOOME**!" I sobbed.

The professor tried to console me.

"Geronimo, listen to this **fun** fact," he said. "Did you know that the largest fossil of dinosaur poop ever found was seventeen inches long and more than six inches wide?"

My cousin **jumped** into the time machine.

"Very interesting fact," Trap said. "Now let's get **out** of here!"

Professor von Volt pressed the **flight** button.

"In sixty seconds, we'll be in Egypt!"

The little ship began to vibrate and fill with a **BLUE MIST**....

LIFE IN ANCIENT EGYPT

In 3000 BC, it is believed that the legendary **King Menes** unified the tribes of Upper and Lower Egypt and began the first of the thirty Egyptian dynasties. This civilization created one of the first forms of writing and the first solar calendar. The ancient Egyptians also made great advances in sculpture, poetry, architecture, mathematics, geometry, and medicine.

The Egyptians depended on the **Nile River** as a source of drinking water and to help them grow crops. The river's periodic floods left the ground rich with **mud** and **lime**, making the soil around the river very fertile.

After every flood, the field's boundaries were redrawn.

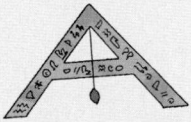

Egyptian engineers used this tool — a plumb bob — in astronomy, navigation, surveying, and building.

The shaduf was one tool used by the Egyptians to water their crops.

A BRIEF HISTORY OF PAPYRUS

PAPYRUS WAS ONE OF THE EARLIEST FORMS OF PAPER. THE PAPYRUS PLANT WAS COMMON AROUND THE NILE RIVER IN ANCIENT EGYPT, AND THE EGYPTIANS USED IT TO CREATE A THICK, PAPERLIKE WRITING MATERIAL. THEY ALSO USED THE PLANT IN THE CONSTRUCTION OF BOATS, MATTRESSES, MATS, ROPES, SANDALS, AND BASKETS.

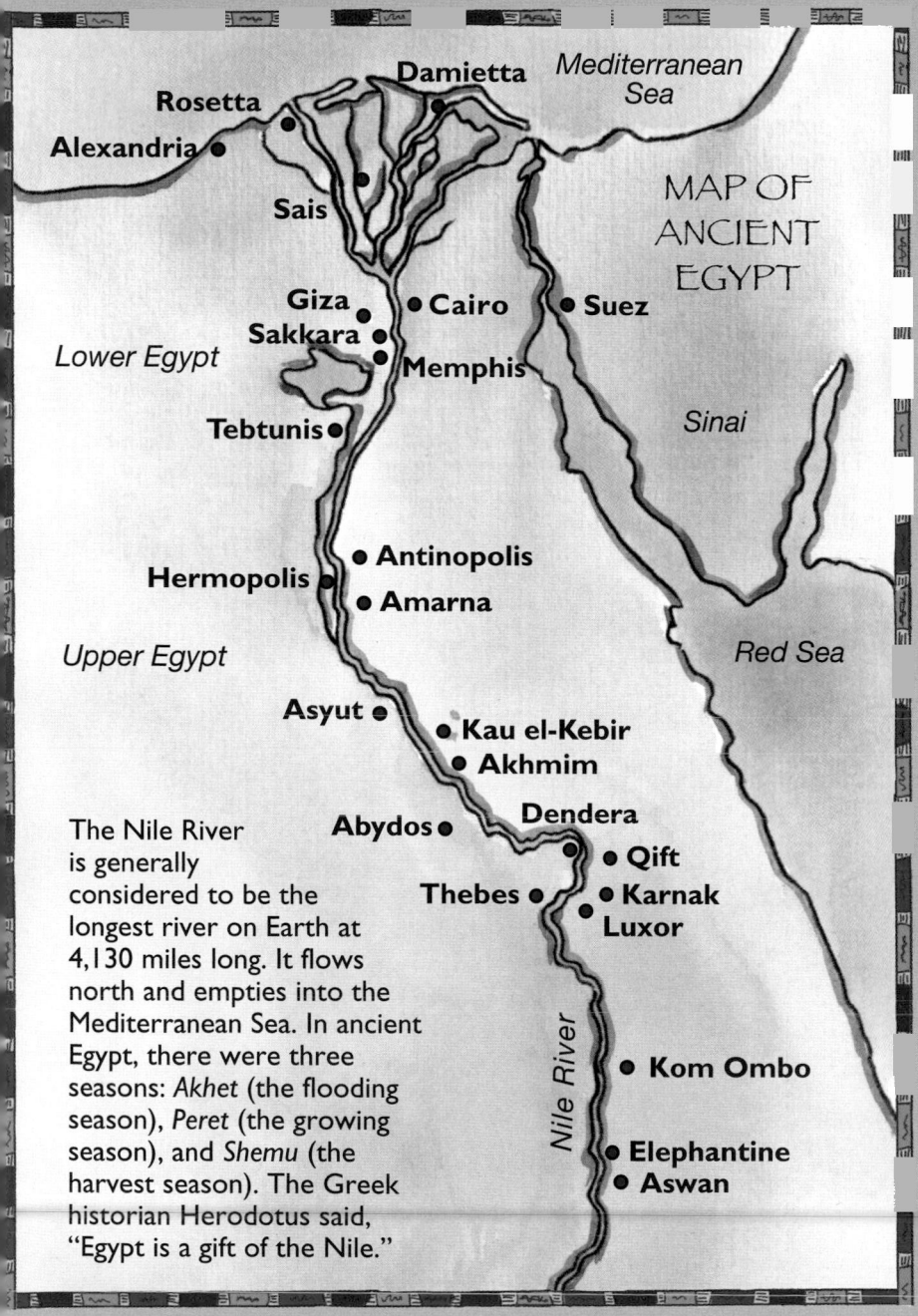

The Nile River is generally considered to be the longest river on Earth at 4,130 miles long. It flows north and empties into the Mediterranean Sea. In ancient Egypt, there were three seasons: *Akhet* (the flooding season), *Peret* (the growing season), and *Shemu* (the harvest season). The Greek historian Herodotus said, "Egypt is a gift of the Nile."

IN THE SHADOW OF THE SPHINX

I plugged my ears, gritted my teeth, and closed my eyes.

Bang! The **MOUSE MOVER 3000** stopped moving. I perked up my ears, but I didn't hear anything. I leaned over and very **slowwwwwwly** opened the porthole.

"**WOW!**" Professor von Volt shouted.

"**WOW!**" I shouted.

"WOW!" Thea shouted.

"WOW!" Benjamin shouted.

"SWEET!" Trap shouted.

The Egyptian desert stretched for miles and miles in every direction around us. It was a sea of golden sand as fine as powder, gently shaped into softly angled dunes. The rising sun tinged the pyramids and the Sphinx with a rosy hue.

"Look!" Benjamin exclaimed in AMAZEMENT. "The pyramids are white and have golden tips! And the Sphinx is painted in different colors!"

I made a note in my travel journal: *It is 1280*

Egyptian society was arranged in this hierarchy.

BC at 5:47 A.M. We're in Giza, in the middle of the Egyptian desert.

The professor rummaged in his pockets and took out some teeny-tiny clothes.

"This is what we'll wear while we're in Egypt!" he told us. "I put these clothes through a special *miniaturization* process before we left."

He took from his pocket a little test tube full of **transparent** liquid and used an eyedropper to splash one drop of the strange substance on a little piece of clothing. The tiny dress **grew** into a pleated linen dress, complete with a wig.

The professor gave it to Thea, along with a small GILDED wooden box. In it were **expensive** perfumes and alabaster vases filled with ancient Egyptian makeup.

After we dressed, Thea put eye makeup on all of us. Now we really looked like **ancient Egyptians**!

I noticed Trap put something in his bag. It

looked like a little **BLACK** fabric pouch.

"Oh!" the professor exclaimed suddenly, slapping his forehead. "I almost forgot!" He took out a tiny earpiece. "This is a **Squeak Speak**, a special translator I invented," he told us. "It can translate everything you hear and all that you say!"

Trap popped a **Squeak Speak** in his ear. "It doesn't work." he said. "I don't hear anything!"

"Of course you don't!" Professor von

EGYPT

MAKEUP

Egyptians applied makeup around their eyes for aesthetic reasons and to protect themselves from the sun's rays and from damage from the sandy desert winds. The most popular colors were black and green. The Egyptians mixed a blue-gray mineral called galena with soot to make black eye makeup. Green eye makeup was made from malachite, a bright green copper ore.

Volt replied with a **sigh**. "You have to turn it on first!"

Trap turned on the device. "One, two, three, **TESTIII

von Volt replied. "According to the ancient Egyptians, the whole world follows the law of universal order and balance. And Ra is the sun god the Egyptians adored."

We hid the **MOUSE MOVER 3000** in a hole in the sand and covered it with palm leaves. Then we got to work. Thea snapped some **PHOTOS**, I took NOTES, and Benjamin and the professor took samples of sand and sealed them in plastic bags. Trap lay **LAZILY** in the shadow of the Sphinx, napping.

After an hour, we were all done.

"Where are we going for breakfast?" Trap asked, **YAWNING** loudly. "I just can't get moving without a nice cup of **COFFEE** in the morning!"

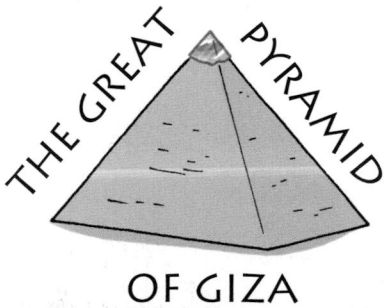

Suddenly, we heard a noise. We ran and hid behind the **GREAT PYRAMID OF GIZA**.

ANCIENT EGYPTIAN GODS

Nephthys, goddess of death

Nut, goddess of the sky

Geb, god of the Earth

Atum, the first god

Shu, god of air

Tefnut, goddess of rain

Khnum, god of rebirth and creation

Anubis, god of the afterlife

Sekhmet, warrior goddess

Ra, sun god

Sobek, crocodile god

Thoth, ibis god

Khepri, god of the scarab beetle

Hathor, goddess of motherhood

Set, god of the desert

Bastet, cat goddess

Osiris, god of the afterlife

Isis, goddess of nature and magic

Horus, god of war and hunting

ARREST THOSE RODENTS!

A **LOOOOOONG** procession of soldiers carrying a **golden** litter with silky curtains came into view.

"Make way for the Grand Vizier, the **NOBLE MOUSEHOTEP**!" the soldiers shouted.

The curtains parted, and I glimpsed a sly-looking, shifty-eyed rat. He was wearing a white linen robe and a blue lapis lazuli necklace decorated with a large gold scarab beetle. He wore a black wig woven with silver threads and pearls, and his tail was decorated with rings made of precious stones.

His servants placed the litter gently on the ground, and the rat climbed out of the *ornate*

chair. A servant ran to him and placed a pair of **golden** sandals on his paws.

Mousehotep nibbled DAINTILY on a bunch of grapes. Meanwhile, Trap took out a piece of garlic chewing gum and waved it in front of my nose.

"Want some?" he whispered.

"Shhh!" I shushed him. "You know I'm allergic to garlic. Ah . . . ah . . . ah . . . **achoo**!"

I sneezed.

The Noble Mousehotep heard me.

"**Scampering scarabs!**" he cried. "Arrest those rodents! They are tomb thieves. Scribe, write that down!"

The soldiers surrounded us, poking at us with their **SPEARS**, while the scribe **SCRIBBLED** something on a piece of papyrus.

RAMESSES! RAMESSES! RAMESSES!

The head guard forced us to march through the extremely HOT desert for what seemed to be an **eternity**! Finally, we arrived at the royal palace of Memphis.

The guard **poked** me in the tail with his lance.

"Bow before the pharaoh!" he ordered me.

At the very far end of the great hall, which was

RAMESSES II (RAMESSES THE GREAT)
(REIGNED FROM 1279–1212 BC)

His name is sometimes written as *Rameses* or *Ramses*, and he was the son of Seti I. He built more large statues of himself than any other pharaoh.

He fought against the Hittites in the battle of Kadesh. Like all ancient Egyptian pharaohs, Ramesses II had many wives, but his favorite and his first chief queen was Nefertari. He boasted that he was the father of more than ninety children, and he lived to be at least ninety years old.

Ramesses in hieroglyphics

decorated in MAGNIFICENT frescoes, I saw a golden throne.

A tall, thin rodent with a hooked nose and hawk-like eyes sat on the throne. It was Ramesses II!

Two tall mice stood on either side of the throne, fanning the pharaoh with ENORMOUSE ostrich feathers. The pharaoh wore a double crown — part red, part white — symbolizing his dominion over Upper and Lower Egypt. He proudly held a gold scepter in his paw.

Queen Nefertari was seated next to him. She was gorgeous! He looked at her proudly; you could tell he was very much in love with her. Next to the royal couple was their daughter. In her arms, she held a little bundle wrapped in a blanket EMBROIDERED in gold. It was the little baby Moses*!

The pharaoh's daughter with little baby Moses

* In Hebrew, *Moses* means "savior" or "drawn out from the water." In Egyptian, it means "son" or "child."

NOBLE MOUSEHOTEP'S SARCOPHAGUS

Grand Vizier Mousehotep **BOWED** before Ramesses.

"Honor to you, **Pharaoh**!" he squeaked. "I wish you life, strength, and health!"

Then he turned to the scribe. "Read!" he ordered.

The scribe read **aloud**:

"HIGH PHARAOH , SON OF THE SUN , RA'S PRIDE , I SURPRISED THESE FIVE RODENTS BEHIND THE PYRAMID OF CHEOPS. THEY ARE MUMMY THIEVES. LET'S FEED THEM TO THE CROCODILES !"

The pharaoh stared at us with a look of FIRE in his eyes. When he finally spoke, his voice was so deep and scary it made me shiver with fright!

"Is this true?" he asked us.

Professor von Volt stepped forward and bowed.

"Noble Ramesses II, we are innocent!" he said.

The Noble Mousehotep laughed an EVIL laugh.

"INNOCENT?" he scoffed. "Everyone says that. To the crocodiles, I say! Did you get that, scribe?"

The scribe chuckled.

"I got it, boss!" he replied.

But the pharaoh lifted a paw.

"If you're not THIEVES, then what are you?" he asked us.

"Pharaoh Ramesses, we are TRAVELERS from afar,"

WOMEN

Women had a lot of liberty in ancient Egypt compared to many early societies: They could work and choose whom to wed. Women could even be pharaohs — Hatshepsut, the fifth pharaoh of the eighteenth dynasty, was female and is thought to have been one of the most successful pharaohs in ancient Egypt.

The pharaoh's dinner
Musicians
Dancers
Scrolls of papyrus
Scribe
Mousehotep
Pool
Guards

Servants
Nefertari
Ramesses II

the professor explained. "We have knowledge of many SECRETS. . . ."

"You must be **magicians**!" Nefertari squeaked with excitement.

Trap took advantage of the situation and threw himself at the foot of her Throne.

"Oh yes, we are magicians," he said. "And we're really, really good ones!"

Trap pulled on a black cloak with a silky scarlet lining. Then he rummaged around in his mysterious satin pouch. He clapped his paws, and instantly a WHITE dove appeared out of thin air and settled on Nefertari's shoulders.

The queen squeaked with delight.

Next, Trap produced a top hat. Out of the hat POPPED two tiny white rabbit ears.

"You get back in there," Trap grunted. "I don't want you yet!"

It turned out that Trap's satin pouch contained everything a mouse needed for a **magic show**!

"Come one, come all," Trap shouted loudly. "Come be amazed by the magic of the **Great** and **Powerful** Trappolik Who Came from Afar! He'll make objects mysteriously **appear** and **disappear**, and he will saw in half the most reckless volunteer — er, I mean, ahem, the most **courageous** volunteer!"

He waved a silk scarf in front of the pharaoh's scepter, and it disappeared instantly! Six soldiers rushed toward him, but in an instant, Trap made the scepter **appear** again.

"**VOILA!**" Trap squeaked triumphantly.

Everyone held their breath.

Then Ramesses chuckled. **"HEE, HEE, HEE!"**

Everyone **laughed** with him. "Hee, hee, hee!"

"I need a box!" Trap squeaked loudly. "Never mind, I found one."

He dragged a **sarcophagus** covered in gold and precious stones in front of the throne.

"You're about to see the world's most **SPECTACULAR** demonstration!" Trap announced boldly.

"Hey!" the Noble Mousehotep protested. "Let go of that sarcophagus. It's mine! And it's very precious!"

But Ramesses nodded for Trap to continue with the show.

Mousehotep began to **sob** uncontrollably.

"That sarcophagus cost me a **FORTUNE**!"

he whined. "Write that down, scribe!"

"Got it, boss!" the scribe replied.

"Ladies and gentlemice, I will now saw my cousin in **HALF**," Trap announced. "Oh, what am I saying? I'm going to saw him in **THIRDS**, no, in **QUARTERS**. Yes, quarters. After all, I'm feeling **good** today."

I began to **sweat** profusely.

"Why me?" I squeaked.

Trap pulled me by the tail.

"Oh, come on," he insisted. "You've got the **easiest** part!"

Then he tripped me and locked me in the sarcophagus.

"**HELP!**" I yelled. "I'm afraid of closed spaces. Trap, let me out, I tell you! I'm **CLAUSTROPHOBIC**!"

"Oh, you'll be fine!" Trap

replied with a chuckle. "Don't you trust me?"

"Of course not!" I mumbled from inside the sarcophagus, but Trap didn't hear me.

He began sawing and whistling at the same time.

"Don't worry, Geronimo," Trap said. "I've tried this trick a DOZEN times. It almost always works!"

After a few seconds, Trap stopped sawing. "Voila!" he announced. "I've sliced my cousin!"

I reached down to feel my tail. I was still INTACT!

Trap opened the sarcophagus and I jumped out. I was as pale as a slice of **mozzarella**. The court applauded with enthusiasm.

"**Bravoooo!**" the mice shouted. "More! More!"

"Pharaoh, who's going to fix my sarcophagus?" Mousehotep demanded as he wiped his tears.

"Quiet!" Ramesses hissed. "Don't bother the **GREAT** and **Powerful** Trappolik Who Came from Afar!"

"Yeah!" Trap agreed with a nod of his head. "Don't bother the **Great** and **POWERFUL** Trappolik Who Came from Afar!"

Mousehotep glared at my cousin.

"By all the sphinxes in Egypt, I'll get you!" he grumbled under his breath. **"WRITE THAT DOWN, SCRIBE!"**

"Got it, boss!" the scribe replied.

THE SECRET OF HIEROGLYPHICS

The ancient Egyptians wrote by using **ideograms** (designs that represent different concepts), and **phonograms** (signs that represent different sounds). Here are a few examples:

These symbols were called **hieroglyphics**. In ancient Egypt, not everyone knew how to write. It was a difficult skill to learn, and those who could do it (the **scribes**) had great power. In 1822, **Jean-François Champollion** was able to decipher the hieroglyphics on the **Rosetta Stone**. The stone had the same text carved in three different languages: ancient Egyptian hieroglyphics, Demotic script, and ancient Greek.

Rosetta Stone

Scribe at work

This is how you write *Geronimo* in Egyptian: 

Now use the key on the next page to try to write your own name!

EGYPTIAN ALPHABET

In reality, there was no Egyptian alphabet. This is an approximation of what the Egyptian alphabet might have looked like.

A	J	S
B	K	T
C	L	U
D	M	V
E	N	W
F	O	X
G	P	Y
H	Q	Z
I	R	

EGYPTIAN NUMBERS

1		10		100		1,000	
2		20		200		10,000	
3		30		300		100,000	
4		40		400		1,000,000	

OOOOOOOOOH . . . MAGIC!

The pharaoh had been so impressed with Trap's magic show that he invited us to stay instead of throwing us to the **crocodiles**. The Egyptians were about to have a **FEAST**.

"Let the celebration in honor of Hapi begin!" Ramesses announced.

I realized he was referring to the flooding of the Nile River, which the Egyptians revered and called **HAPI**.

The priests dressed all in white and lit sticks of perfumed incense. Seven dancers wearing **golden-threaded** wigs and **LAPIS LAZULI** necklaces entered the great hall. They danced as they shook the sistrum and tossed rose petals into the air. Then they somersaulted gracefully around

The sistrum was an ancient Egyptian percussion instrument.

the pool in the center of the hall, which was filled with water lilies.

Meanwhile, the musicians played **sweet** melodies on the harp, cithara, lyre, lute, castanets, and tambourines.

The servants set out a meal of **QUAIL**, roasted meat, goat cheese, **spicy** beans, pomegranates, grapes, **caramelized** nuts, honey, and fig marmalade on alabaster dishes.

Ramesses popped a honey treat in his mouth. Suddenly, he groaned in **pain**.

"Oh, ouch!" he cried. "**Ouchie**! Ouchie! Ouch!"

"Poor **dear**, does your tooth ache?" Nefertari **SQUEAKED**.

MEDICINE

Egyptian doctors knew how to mend bone fractures, how to drill into the skull, and how to perform complicated surgeries. They also cured some illnesses with certain types of mold, which is the active ingredient in modern-day penicillin. The Egyptians filled cavities with a special cement and tied false teeth to real ones with golden threads.

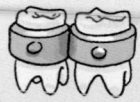

"Oh, yes," he sighed, rubbing his cheek. "I've really got to go to the dentist!"

The festivities were about to begin, and a servant brought Nefertari a **golden** mirror studded with **RUBIES** so she could freshen her makeup.

Unfortunately, the mirror was clouded over and couldn't **REFLECT** very much.

Trap took note of this and rummaged around in his pouch. He took out a sparkling new mirror. Then he bowed down and offered it to the queen. She gasped in wonder.

"Ooooooooh . . . magic!" she exclaimed.

Nefertari gave Trap the **SWEETEST** smile.

"He's phenomenal. . . ." I heard one of the other mice whisper.

"A **TRUE** magician, and a whisker-licking good one at that," another replied.

EGYPT

CLOTHING

Wealthy Egyptians wore pleated linen skirts and tunics that were tinted with vegetable dye, while shepherds and farmers wore tunics made of rough animal skins. Tunics were rarely made of wool. The rich wore leather sandals, while the poor wore sandals made of woven straw.

"It seems he comes from very far away," a third whispered. "He must be very powerful."

"Yes, very powerful," the first agreed. "Maybe more powerful than the pharaoh . . ."

"Mm-hmmm," the second said. "The queen smiled at him. . . ."

"Ramesses must be so jealous!" another chimed in.

Mummified mozzarella! We were in big trouble if those mice were correct. It wasn't a good idea to make the pharaoh jealous. Mousehotep whispered something in the pharaoh's ear. Ramesses NARROWED his eyes and curled the tips of his mustache in a way that made my whiskers tremble in fear.

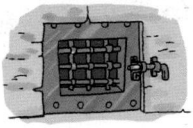

OUCH! WHO PINCHED ME?

Ramesses stormed out of the hall looking very, very **ANGRY**. Mousehotep followed closely behind, whispering to Ramesses and shooting us **dirty looks**.

I knew it! I knew we were in **trouble**!

"I told you the pharaoh was jealous. . . ." I heard a mouse murmur.

"It serves that **magician** right!" said another.

"Mm-hmmm," agreed a third. "Ramesses will feed him to the crocodiles for sure!"

"By tomorrow, the only thing left of him and his

friends will be their TINY LITTLE BONES!"

Holey cheese! We were doomed!

Mousehotep came running into the main hall. "Guards, imprison the strangers!" he shouted with delight. "Pharaoh's orders!"

Before I could SQUEAK a reply, we were surrounded. The guards poked us with their lances and we were led to the palace's DUNGEON.

"Hee, hee, hee!" Mousehotep chuckled. "You thought you were being so CLEVER, but now you'll pay DEARLY for your insolence."

He poked Trap's chubby tummy.

"Oh, yes!" he cackled. "The King of the Sacred Crocodiles is going to love you!"

"Look here," my cousin protested, placing a paw

on his round belly. "This is pure MUSCLE!"

Trap, Thea, Benjamin, Professor von Volt, and I settled into our dank, dark cell.

I climbed up on the lone WOODEN bench and looked out the small prison window. Right in front of me was a muddy pool of water. In it swam gigantic, hungry-looking crocodiles.

Why, why, oh, why had I agreed to come on this wacky journey through time?

Suddenly, something pinched my tail.

"Ouch!" I exclaimed. "Who's that? Who's there? Who pinched me?"

It wasn't the pharaoh's soldiers, but a LOVELY maiden.

"Shhh!" she whispered. "Follow me, all of you. And be quiet!"

We scurried away through a DARK passageway. SMOKY torches cast an eerie glow on the walls,

which were covered in hieroglyphics. The maiden led us to an enormouse statue of Sobek, the **frightening** crocodile god. She pressed the statue's left paw, and the statue revolved to reveal a **SECRET** door.

We **followed** the maiden through the door and found ourselves in the queen's **PRIVATE** chambers!

Nefertari **RAN** toward us, a **worried** look on her snout.

"You have to get away!" she said urgently. "The pharaoh is **very** jealous!"

"But why are you helping us?" Thea asked the queen *suspiciously*.

Nefertari turned **PURPLE** with embarrassment.

"Sometimes the pharaoh can be a real bully," she admitted. "He's especially **GRUMPY** right now because of his awful toothache. You seem like decent mice. You should have a chance to **ESCAPE**."

"Thank you," I told her gratefully. "We will remember your **kindness**."

The queen removed one of her **PRECIOUS** rings and gave it to Trap.

"Here," she told him. "This ring will protect you. **Travel safely!**"

LET'S GO! ROOOOOOOOOW!

The maiden told us to lie down on a giant woven rug. Then she **rolled** up the rug, hiding us inside. Some servants carried us straight to the port in Memphis. It was already five o'clock in the afternoon.

"Crusty cheese curds!" Trap mumbled. "I missed lunch. I don't like this at all!"

I heard the sound of waves lapping against the shore. I stuck my snout out of the rug. We had been loaded onto a felucca, a small wooden boat propelled by oars and sails.

"Mummified mozzarella and

petrified papyrus!" we heard an **ANGRY** voice shout. "This is the laziest crew since Atum created Egypt! We have to get up the Nile before sunset. Let's go! **ROOOOOOOW!**"

Captain Sewer al-Rati was a **MUSCULAR** rat with **curly** whiskers. He wore a rough linen skirt and wide leather bracelets on his wrists.

"One pyramid, two pyramids, three pyramids, **ROW**! One pyramid, two pyramids, three pyramids, **ROW**!"

Everyone rowed vigorously. The ship left the Memphis port and began to sail down the river. I was **green** with seasickness. The boat went **UP** and **DOWN**, **UP** and **DOWN**, and **UP** and **DOWN**. I felt like I was going to toss my cheese!

Why, why, oh, why had I agreed to come on this wacky journey through time?

LOOK OUT FOR HIPPOS!

We had been traveling for several hours, and night had fallen.

Suddenly, a sailor shouted: "Look out for hippopotamuses!"

Hippopotamuses? What hippopotamuses?

Another sailor shouted, "Petrified papyrus! They're **ENORMOUSE**! And there are a lot of them!"

I felt faint. *Enormouse hippos?*

Captain Sewer al-Rati thundered: "Scampering scarabs . . . WE'RE SINKING!"

My whiskers twisted from fright. SINKING?

Suddenly, the ship began to tilt wildly to one side.

"Mummified mozzarella!" I squeaked. "We'll be **dinner** for those hungry hippos!"

Why, why, oh, why had I agreed to come on this wacky journey through time?

A huge wave crashed against the side of the boat. The boat was filling with water ***fast***.

I grabbed a basket full of fish and **dumped** them overboard. Then I started scooping up basketfuls of water.

"Hurry," I urged my friends. "We have to bail out the boat!"

But it was no use. The water just seeped out the sides of the basket!

"Farewell, friends!" I cried out to the professor, Trap, Thea, and Benjamin. "We're

SNIP, SNIP, SNAP!

A moment later, I found myself in the **muddy** waters of the Nile River. I fumbled and thrashed, trying to keep my snout above **water**. But my soaked linen garment was pulling me down.

"**Crusty cheese curds**," I heard my cousin grumble. "Now I've missed **dinner**, too!"

In the light of the full moon, I saw lots of shiny dots **SHIMMERING** in the dark. Trembling, I realized they were **CROCODILE** eyes!

"Crocs!" I yelled to my friends. "Swim!"

With the crocodiles nipping at our tails, we swam toward the shore. **SNIP, SNIP, SNAP!**

One of the crocodiles **BIT** Trap on the tail.

"Ouchie, ouchie, ouch!" Trap yelled. He

grabbed an oar and waved it at the crocodile.

The crocodile snapped at Trap.

Trap poked the crocodile with the oar and began to sing.

"Stay back, stay back, you crusty old croc!
You smell like a pair of three-day-old socks.
Your sickening smell is worse than your bite.
So go away, scram — get out of our sight!"

ANIMALS

The ancient Egyptians were some of the earliest people to keep domesticated animals. Many amulets worn by Egyptians were shaped like animals, and some gods, such as Bastet (the cat goddess), Anubis (the jackal-headed god), and Sobek (the crocodile god), had the heads of animals. The Egyptians also attributed magical powers to cats, and mummified cats were often found in tombs. Cats in Egypt were called *miu*, which meant "he or she who mews."

cat mummy

THE BEST NIGHT OF MY LIFE!

Luckily, we made it to shore. The moonlight **illuminated** the white beach, and the thick papyrus growing along the shore **SWAYED** in the night breeze. Suddenly, I saw a shadow among the papyrus fronds, and something hit me on the head. ***Bonk!***

OOOOOUCHIE! WHAT A BLOW, WHAT A WHACK, WHAT A WALLOP!

As I passed out, I heard Trap **grumbling** in the background.

"Geronimo is always the same," he said. "He'll do anything to get attention. There he goes, fainting again!"

EGYPT

CHILDREN

Egyptian children were very loved by their parents. They played with balls, tops, rag dolls, and wooden animals. Boys and girls usually had shaved heads and side braids.

A few seconds later, I came to. A **tiny** figure stood in front of me. It was a little mouse about the same age as Benjamin.

She had a shaved head except for a thick braid that was decorated with a little PAINTED wooden ball. She wore an antelope skin that was tied at her waist by a BRAIDED leather belt.

"Are you still alive?" she squeaked anxiously. "I'm so sorry! I hit you with my **throwing stick**!"

Professor von Volt was scribbling notes.

"Interesting," he mused. "This Egyptian throwing stick is identical to the boomerang used by Australian Aboriginals!"

Pa-rat Riri-rat Ma-rat

The little mouse told us her name was Riri-rat. She took us to a mud hut where her parents welcomed us **WARMLY**. Pa-rat invited us to stay.

"No one in my village will ever go through the night **hungry**!" he said, using an ancient Egyptian proverb.

"It's about time we had something to **eat**!" Trap announced as he patted his belly and licked his lips.

The family offered us everything they had with a **smile**: dried fish, fresh cucumbers, fava beans with garlic, barley cakes made with sesame oil, goat cheese, and ripe, juicy figs.

We sat in a circle on WOVEN mats and ate the food with our paws.

After we ate, the adult mice played **senet** while Benjamin and Riri-rat played with a toy maze. Even though we were in a mud hut LIT by an oil lamp almost 3,300 years in the past, it was the ***best*** night of my life. The food was simple and delicious, and it was offered with **warmth** and generosity!

We chatted about many things and made the most of the PEACEFUL, relaxing evening.

I turned to our hosts.

"Friends, tomorrow we must secretly return to Giza," I told them. "We've escaped our captors, but we need to complete our mission."

Benjamin looked sad about leaving.

Senet was a game similar to backgammon. It was played on a rectangular board with thirty-six squares.

Benjamin and Riri-rat's maze

"The memory of this charming night will live in our **hearts** forever!" I assured everyone.

Even though we were very different from Riri-rat and her family, we were united by friendship. It was **comforting** to know that no matter how far we had traveled through time, we had found true friends who had warmed our hearts with their hospitality.

There is no greater gift than friendship!

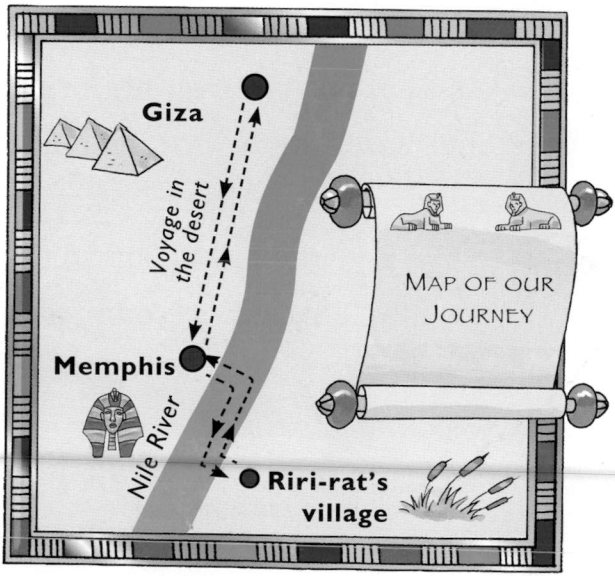

THE MUMMY'S CAFÉ

That night, we slept on pallets made of **DRIED** grass. At dawn, we went down to the river with Pa-rat and helped him bring in the night's catch: a netful of **fish**. We explained to him that we had to quickly return to Memphis and from there, travel back to Giza. We also told him no one was to know of our plans. If Ramesses or Mousehotep found us, we would be in **BIG** trouble!

Pa-rat put his paw over his **heart**.

"You have my word of honor," he squeaked. "I will be as silent as an **OBELISK**! But you'll need a guide."

Suddenly, a small, chubby fisherman appeared from behind a dune. He had a **sly** look on his snout.

"Oh, oh!" Pa-rat whispered. "That's

Obelisk

Chatty al-Mousi, the town gossip!"

Chatty cleared his throat.

"Erhem," he said. "Pardon me, but I was just passing by when I heard you needed a **guide**. My brother's cousin's uncle's maid's niece's scribe's sister's embalmer's grandfather is a tourist guide in Memphis. His name is **BAB-BEOT**. You'll find him at the port, at **THE MUMMY'S CAFÉ**. I'll send him a carrier pigeon to let him know you're coming."

Since we didn't have any other options, we agreed. Pa-rat helped us build a **boat**. We would glide up the Nile to Memphis.

Just as we were about to leave, Riri-rat gave Benjamin her throwing stick.

"It's the most **valuable** thing I have," she told him. "That's why I want to give it to you.

We gathered and cut lots of papyrus plants and tied them together with sturdy knots to make a boat.

I wish you a peaceful and safe journey."

She kissed him sweetly on the cheek. Benjamin's snout turned **PURPLE** with embarrassment. He's a **shy** mouse, just like me. We boarded the boat and waved good-bye. The boat slowly **glided** on the river.

After a few hours, the current began to **whirl**. We were getting closer and closer to the rapids. The boat began to pick up **SPEED**.

"We should slow down!" I yelled to Trap.

"No way!" Trap replied. "You're such a **scaredy**-mouse. Now comes the fun part!"

He steered the boat right into the rapids.

"Wheeeeeeeeeee!" he shouted.

As I was tossed UP and DOWN and UP and DOWN and UP and DOWN among the waves, panic took hold of me. I grabbed the sides of the boat. Suddenly, a branch fell off a tree near the shore. It hit me on the head. BONK!

Oooooouchie! What a blow, what a whack, what a wallop!

As I passed out, I heard Trap grumbling in the background.

"Geronimo is always the same," he said. "He'll do anything to get attention. Look, he fainted again!"

The evening of the second day, we arrived in Memphis. We tied up the boat right near the

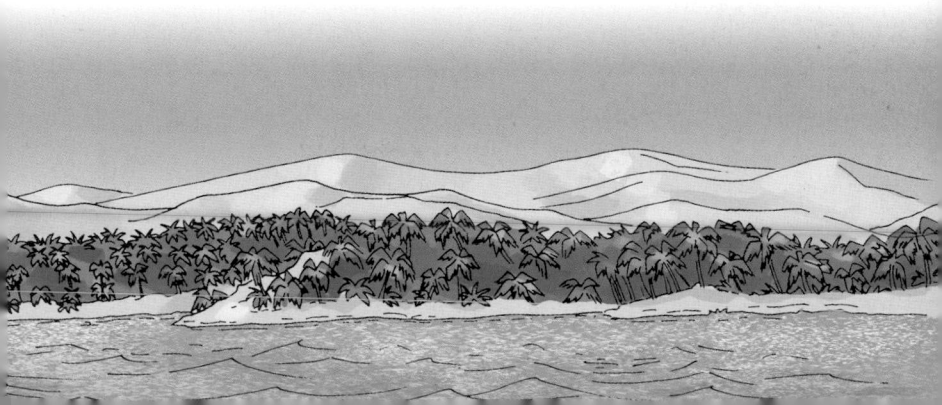

entrance to the port.

Then we quickly made our way to the Mummy's Café.

When we entered, a short, skinny, bald rat greeted us. He shouted loudly.

"Hi, there!" he said. "Are you the ones who want to go to Giza?"

The professor tried to QUIET him.

"Shhh!" he said. "Please speak SOFTLY or we'll be discovered!"

"Discovered?" he shouted back, louder than before. "Discover what? Is there a SECRET? A very secret secret? Huh? Is there?"

We ushered him to a quiet table in the back of the café, hoping no one had heard him.

"My name is BAB-BEOT," he introduced himself. "It means 'brain lice of the desert.' But I have other names, too. Like

Kiak-Kie-Rom, which means 'My tongue is longer than that of a horned viper.' I'm also known as **Mum-Puz**, which means 'My paws stink worse than a rotting mummy,' as well as **Atten al-Alit**, or 'My breath is fouler than that of a garlic-eating jackal.'"

Professor von Volt took a step backward. The guide truly had **stinky** breath.

"Ahem, can we get going?" Thea asked. "We're in a hurry to get to Giza."

"Don't you want to first go on a *beautiful* cruise down the Nile?" the guide asked us.

"No, thank you," Benjamin replied. "We want to go to Giza!"

"You could visit the tomb of King —"

"Maybe another time," Thea replied PATIENTLY. "We want to go to Giza!"

"Want to see the Temple of Ptah? There's a golden statue of Seti I, our pharaoh's dad. . . ."

"Nope!" Trap replied in frustration. "We want to go to Giza! G-i-z-a! GIZAAAAAAAAAA!"

"Oh, you want to go to Giza?" the guide asked. "Why didn't you say so? All right, let's go to Giza, then. But I don't know what you want to see there. There are only three pyramids and a SPHINX in Giza. But if that's where you want to go, I'll take you. Mummified mozzarella! You only had to say so!"

THE TEMPLE OF THE EMBALMERS

We left the café to find mice had gathered in the street to celebrate. We had made it to Memphis just in time. The Nile River had begun to overflow, and everyone was celebrating since the FLOODING guarantees an abundant harvest.

Bab-beot signaled us to follow him.

"Let's go," he told us. "Here's the HOUSE OF LIFE, the temple where embalmers prepare the dead for eternal life. Do you want to see it?"

SCAMPERING SCARABS! I didn't want to see any mummies — I'm a big scaredy-mouse!

But he had already opened the heavy door, and I couldn't help but look inside. My head began to spin, and I started to sweat.

"How are you feeling, Uncle?" Benjamin

Sarcophagus
Resins and perfumes
Sacred amulets to be inserted between bandages
Linen bandages
Natron salts

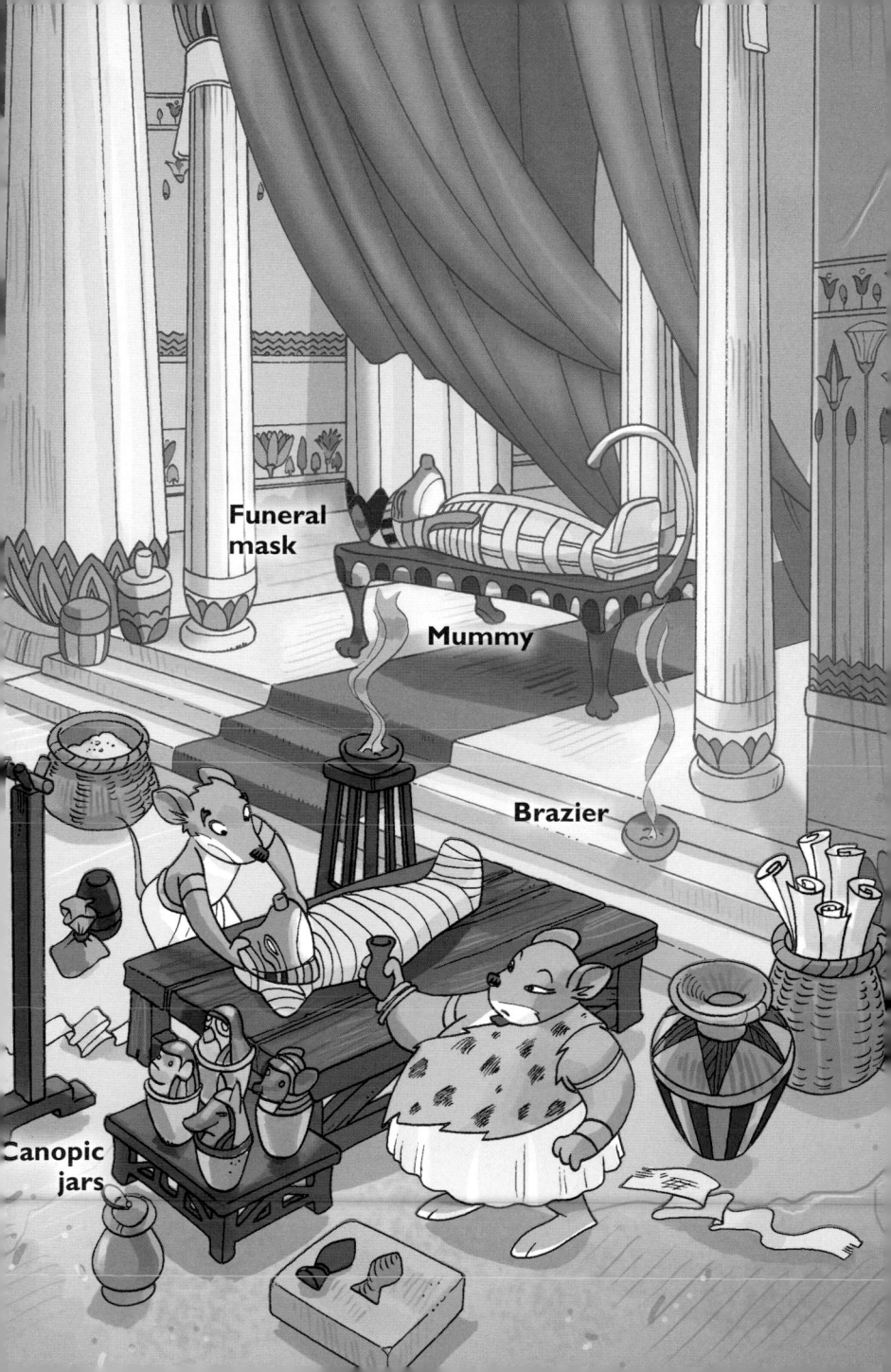
Funeral mask
Mummy
Brazier
Canopic jars

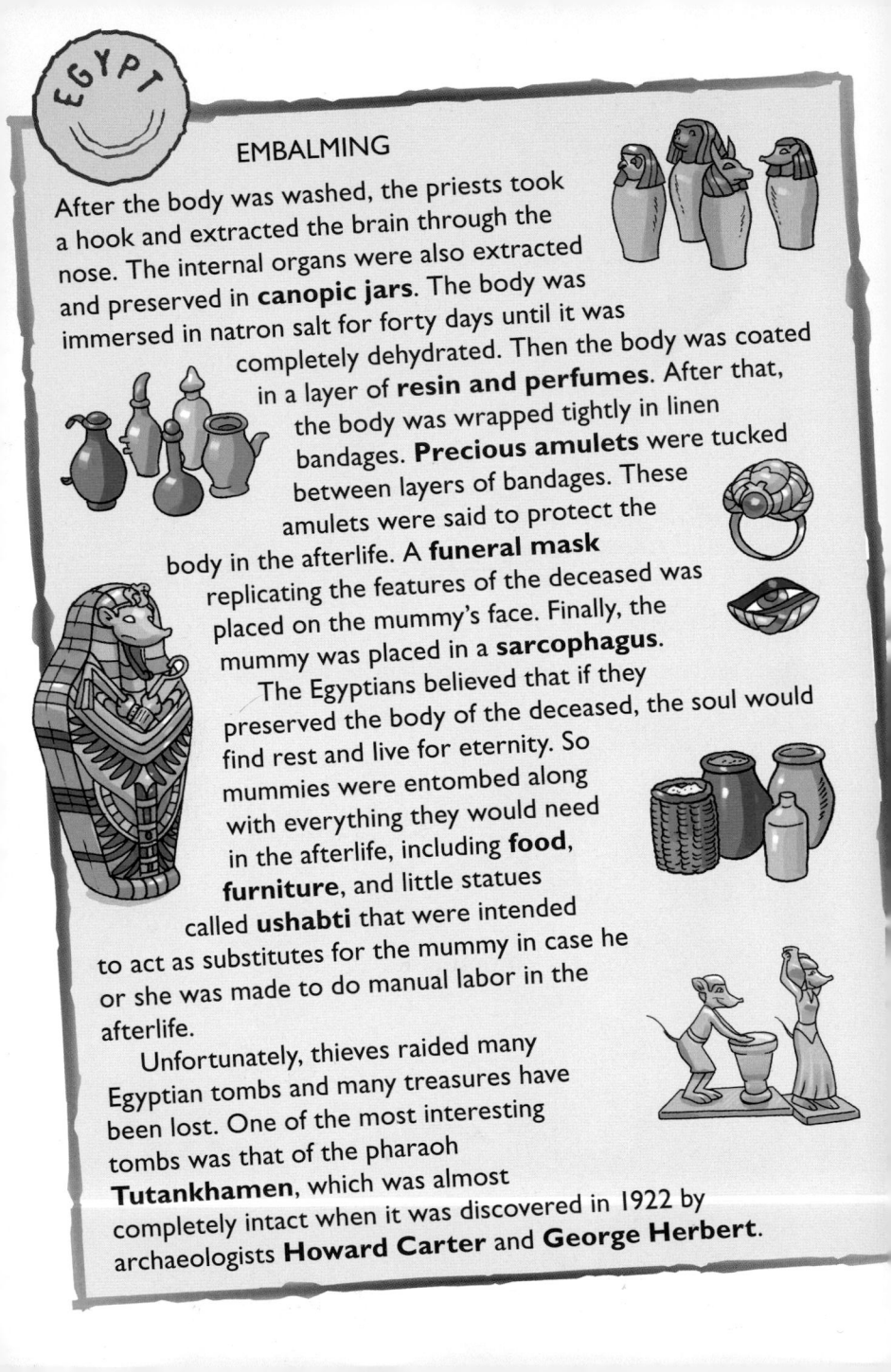

EGYPT

EMBALMING

After the body was washed, the priests took a hook and extracted the brain through the nose. The internal organs were also extracted and preserved in **canopic jars**. The body was immersed in natron salt for forty days until it was completely dehydrated. Then the body was coated in a layer of **resin and perfumes**. After that, the body was wrapped tightly in linen bandages. **Precious amulets** were tucked between layers of bandages. These amulets were said to protect the body in the afterlife. A **funeral mask** replicating the features of the deceased was placed on the mummy's face. Finally, the mummy was placed in a **sarcophagus**.

The Egyptians believed that if they preserved the body of the deceased, the soul would find rest and live for eternity. So mummies were entombed along with everything they would need in the afterlife, including **food**, **furniture**, and little statues called **ushabti** that were intended to act as substitutes for the mummy in case he or she was made to do manual labor in the afterlife.

Unfortunately, thieves raided many Egyptian tombs and many treasures have been lost. One of the most interesting tombs was that of the pharaoh **Tutankhamen**, which was almost completely intact when it was discovered in 1922 by archaeologists **Howard Carter** and **George Herbert**.

whispered. "You're as pale as a slice of **mozzarella**!"

I leaned against a **marble** column. The column tipped over and hit a sarcophagus. Then the lid hit me on the head. **BONK!**

Oooouchie! What a blow, what a whack, what a wallop!

Before I passed out, I heard my cousin's voice.

"Geronimo is always the same," Trap grumbled. "He'll do anything to get attention. There he goes, fainting again!"

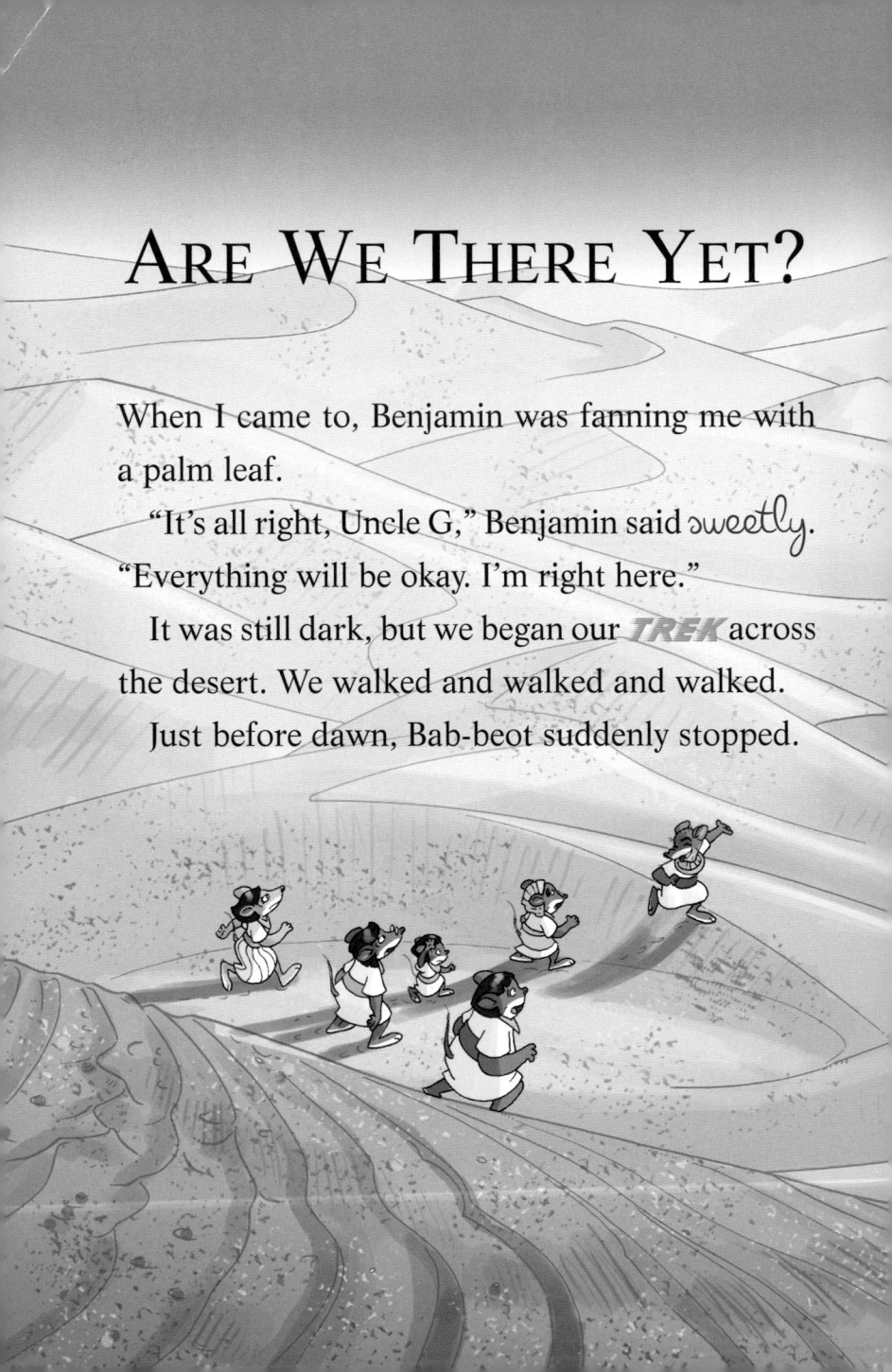

ARE WE THERE YET?

When I came to, Benjamin was fanning me with a palm leaf.

"It's all right, Uncle G," Benjamin said *sweetly*. "Everything will be okay. I'm right here."

It was still dark, but we began our **TREK** across the desert. We walked and walked and walked.

Just before dawn, Bab-beot suddenly stopped.

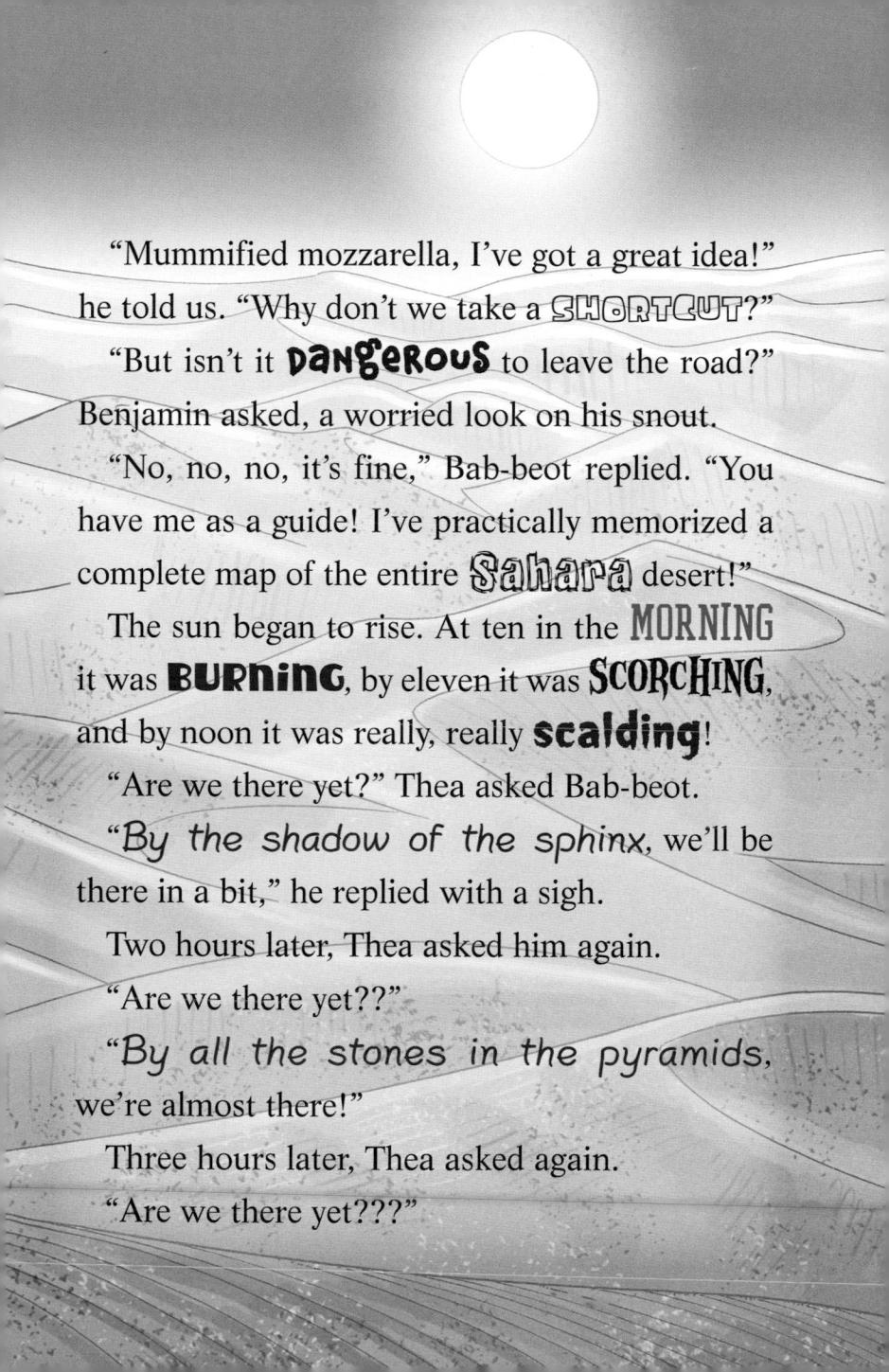

"Mummified mozzarella, I've got a great idea!" he told us. "Why don't we take a SHORTCUT?"

"But isn't it DANGEROUS to leave the road?" Benjamin asked, a worried look on his snout.

"No, no, no, it's fine," Bab-beot replied. "You have me as a guide! I've practically memorized a complete map of the entire Sahara desert!"

The sun began to rise. At ten in the MORNING it was BURNING, by eleven it was SCORCHING, and by noon it was really, really scalding!

"Are we there yet?" Thea asked Bab-beot.

"By the shadow of the sphinx, we'll be there in a bit," he replied with a sigh.

Two hours later, Thea asked him again.

"Are we there yet??"

"By all the stones in the pyramids, we're almost there!"

Three hours later, Thea asked again.

"Are we there yet???"

"*By the light of the rising sun,* we're just about there!"

Thea grabbed Bab-beot by the tail. "We've been here before! I remember this rock!"

Professor von Volt stepped between Thea and our guide.

"Okay, Bab-beot," the professor said politely but firmly. "Tell us the **TRUTH**!"

He burst into tears.

"*By the curly whiskers of the pharaoh's great-grandfather,* I'm afraid I'm lost!"

A tomb-like silence fell over the group. I began to panic, which made me VERY thirsty.

"Trap, please pass me a little water," I whispered.

"WATER?" He paled. "Didn't *you* bring it?"

"No," I replied. "You told me you were going to take care of the provisions."

"I did," Trap said. "I packed the **dried** herring, **salted** beef, and **brined** hot peppers. But I

didn't take any water."

"All salty things?" I shouted back. "And no water? What were you thinking?!"

Why, why, oh, why had I agreed to come on this wacky journey through time?

We took refuge under the shade of the first palm tree we found. Once the SUN had slipped behind the sand dunes, Professor von Volt opened his bag and took out a BRASS instrument.

"It's a SEXTANT. It will be useful for helping us figure out where we are." He pointed the instrument toward the sky.

"We're very close to Giza!" he announced HAPPILY. "Just a few more hours, and we'll be there!"

The sextant is an optical instrument that can measure the distance from the horizon to a star in the sky. This measurement can then be used to determine one's location.

PUT YOUR PAW HERE, COUSIN!

By dawn, we were **exhausted**. We had been walking across the desert for more than twenty-four hours! And we hadn't had a drop of water to drink! Benjamin was slowly **dragging** his little paws through the sand. I hoisted him onto my back and began the trudge again.

"Uncle . . . Uncle Geronimo . . ." he whispered.

"What is it, my little **CHEESE NIP**?" I asked, my mouth bone-dry.

Benjamin didn't answer. He just pointed his finger toward the horizon. I took off my glasses and polished them on the sleeve of my jacket. When I put them back on, I saw something ahead. But what was it? Maybe it was a **MIRAGE**, but I thought I saw the giant sphinx of Giza. And

behind the sphinx was an **OASIS**!

With our last bit of remaining strength, we dragged ourselves toward the cluster of palms, sycamores, and tamarinds, where a spring of CRYSTAL CLEAR water flowed.

"Water . . . water . . . water!" Trap stammered as he dove into the pool of water.

"How's your nephew, Geronimo?" Professor von Volt asked.

"He'll be FINE, Professor," I replied.

I carried Benjamin to the spring and helped him take a drink. Then I gave him a tiny kiss on top of his head.

"We're saved, little one," I told him. "Saved!"

Once he'd had his fill, I took a drink myself. I drank and drank and **drank**. Ah, how good water tastes when one is thirsty!

Once we had all had our fill of water, I realized how **HUNGRY** I was. I could have eaten twenty

WHEELS of cheese all by myself!

Faster than a cat chasing a rat, Trap hopped out of the water and **SCAMPERED** up a palm tree. A minute later, a bunch of dates fell on my head. **Bonk!**

Ooouchie! What a blow, what a whack, what a wallop!

My head began to **spin** and my paws started to **sweat**. As I passed out, I heard my cousin grumbling.

"Geronimo is always the same," Trap said. "He'll do anything to get attention. There he goes, fainting again!"

Finally, I came to.

We were excited to be back in Giza at last. But our good mood was cut short when we heard someone **sobbing** nearby.

"Oh, may the scarabs **save** me!" a voice squeaked. "What will the pharaoh do to me? He'll feed me to the desert jackals!"

PYR-A-MIDION'S SECRET

We followed the voice and found a mouse with a shaved head crying ***desperately***.

"Ahem! Can we help you?" Professor von Volt asked.

The mouse dried a tear on his **elegant** pleated linen tunic and shook his head. The turquoise necklace he wore ***jingled*** as he spoke.

"I'm afraid no mouse can help me," he said with a **SAD** sigh.

"My name is **Pyr-a-midion**." He blew his nose loudly on a palm leaf.

BPRRRRRRRRRR!

"Until a week ago, I was the pharaoh's **GRAND VIZIER**, and my name was respected all over Egypt. I can still hear the people chanting: **Pyr-a-midion! Pyr-a-midion! Pyr-a-midion!** In other words, I was **famouse**. But then . . ."

"But then what?" we all asked together.

Trap sat down in the sand and propped his feet up on a rock.

"I'm gonna make myself comfortable," he grumbled. "Looks like this is going to be a **looooooooong story**!"

"As I was saying," Pyr-a-midion continued, "a week ago, that **SNEAKY**, no-good rodent came to court. In other words — Mousehotep!"

"Mousehotep?!" we all shouted together.

"Yes, yes, Mousehotep," he replied. "He's the one. He's truly, truly **WICKED**! That rascal started to plot against me. And then . . ."

"And then what?" we all asked together.

"And then one week ago, my wife, Pyr-a-midina, made some almond cookies for the pharaoh. 'Be sure they're really, really GOOD!' I warned her. 'I'll put in loads of ALMONDS!' she assured me. And she did. But alas, a TINY fragment of almond shell ended up in one of the cookies. When Ramesses bit into the cookie, he chipped his front tooth! And then . . ."

"And then what?" we all yelled together.

Pyr-a-midion pulled at his whiskers in DESPERATION.

"The pharaoh became FURIOUS! Mousehotep insinuated that I had plotted against the pharaoh and that Pyr-a-midina had left the almond shell in the cookie *on purpose*! Ramesses named *him* Grand Vizier instead

of me. The pharaoh was about to feed me to the crocodiles for dinner when . . ."

"When what?" we all shouted together.

"I knew this was going to be a LOOOOONG story," Trap mumbled.

"My wife threw herself at Nefertari's feet and asked for MERCY," Pyr-a-midion continued. "The queen was moved, and I was given one last chance. But then . . ."

"But then what?" we all yelled together again.

"Then the MALICIOUS Mousehotep suggested the pharaoh give me an extremely DIFFICULT puzzle to solve to gain my freedom. The pharaoh gave me seven days to solve it, and my time is up right NOW. When the sun rises, I'll be breakfast for crocodiles!"

The soldiers that were snoozing in the melon field behind the oasis yawned. They were about to take Pyr-a-midion away!

The prisoner cast a nervous glance at them and shuddered.

"What's the puzzle?" Benjamin asked sweetly. "Maybe we can **help** you solve it."

Pyr-a-midion sighed.

"It's **VERY**, **VERY**, **VERY** difficult," he explained. "In fact, it's impossible to solve. It's

the Riddle of the Sphinx! No mouse has been able to solve it, **ever**!"

? ? ?

THE RIDDLE OF THE SPHINX

THE RIDDLE OF THE SPHINX

WHAT ANIMAL WALKS ON FOUR FEET WHEN HE'S YOUNG, ON TWO FEET WHEN HE'S AN ADULT, AND ON THREE FEET WHEN HE'S OLD?

Pyr-a-midion read the puzzle aloud to us. Then he blew his nose loudly on a palm leaf.

Bprrrrrrrrrrr!

"I've thought about it for seven days and seven NIGHTS, but I haven't come up with

the answer," he sobbed. "What animal first has four feet, then two, and finally three? Oh, may the SCARABS save me!"

Professor von Volt closed his eyes and concentrated. Suddenly, he opened his eyes.

"Aha!" he shouted. "I've got it! It's us! When we're babies, we crawl, which is FOUR feet, when we're adults, we walk on TWO, and when we're old, we lean on a cane, so that becomes THREE feet!"

Pyr-a-midion hugged the professor with glee.

"Oh, thank you!" he told him. "Now I can go back and give Mousehotep the CORRECT answer!"

"I'm going to do you a favor, my friend," Trap said with a chuckle. "I'm going to tell you some *clever* questions you can ask Mousehotep. I guarantee he won't be able to answer them! He'll look bad, and the pharaoh will ask you to be the **Grand Vizier** again."

CLEVER QUESTIONS FOR MOUSEHOTEP

1. A brick weighs one pound plus a half a brick. How much does a brick weigh?
2. If you have ten sarcophagi, and I take all but three, how many sarcophagi are left?
3. Crocodile eggs are hatching in the swamp. The number of crocodiles doubles every minute. After one hour, the swamp is full of crocodiles. After how many minutes was it half full?
4. A sailor is painting a ship on the dock in Memphis. He is standing on a nine-and-a-half-foot ladder. The rungs are eight inches apart. The sailor is standing on the lowest rung, which is twelve inches from the surface of the water. The dock's tide rises three feet every hour. How many rungs does the sailor have to climb to stay dry?
5. A pharaoh has to take a cat, a mouse, and a piece of cheese to Thebes. To get to Thebes, he has to cross the Nile on a boat. There's only room on the boat for the pharaoh and one of the three. If the pharaoh leaves the cat alone with the mouse, or the mouse alone with the cheese, one will eat the other. What should the pharaoh do?
6. The sum of the pharaoh's age, the Grand Vizier's age, and the chief guard's age is eighty-four. In ten years, what will the sum of their ages be?
7. If a choir of twenty mice takes three minutes to sing a song, how many minutes will a choir of ten mice take to sing the same song?

9 Which of the two horizontal lines is longer?

8 Which of the two figures has a bigger area: the black circle or the black ring?

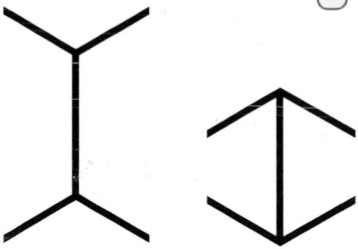

11 Which of these two vertical lines is longer?

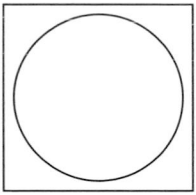

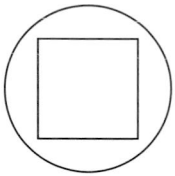

10 Which of these two circles is bigger?

CLEVER ANSWERS

1. Two pounds. 2. Three are left. 3. After 59 minutes. 4. The number of steps out of the water remains the same because the ship goes up with the tide. 5. The pharaoh should take the mouse to Thebes by boat and return empty-handed. He should then take the cat to Thebes and return with the mouse. Then he should take the cheese to Thebes, leave it safely with the cat, and return empty-handed. Finally, he should take the mouse to Thebes. 6. 114 (84+30). 7. Three minutes. 8. The ring has a larger area than the circle. 9. They are the same length. 10. They are the same size. 11. They are the same length.

THE SECRET OF THE GREAT PYRAMID

Pyr-a-midion hugged us.

"Thank you all **SO** much!" he said. "How can I ever make it up to you? Ask for anything you want."

The professor put a paw on his shoulder.

"Dear Pyr-a-midion, it was our **pleasure** to help you," he said.

"Hey, Professor," Trap whispered. "Ask him how the **pyramids** are built!"

"Ahem, there is something," the professor said. "As a scholar, I would like to know how the pyramids are built."

"That is a **very** interesting question!" Pyr-a-midion replied with a chuckle.

Thea surreptitiously snapped a splendid **PHOTO**

with the Sphinx in the background as Professor von Volt began taking notes.

EGYPT

THE GREAT SPHINX OF GIZA

This famous statue has the body of a lion and the head of a man. It is 241 feet long, 66 feet high, and 63 feet wide, and was carved from a single piece of limestone. Experts believe the Sphinx was originally painted in bright colors.

Professor von Volt's Notes

Egyptologists believe the Great Pyramid of Giza was built as a tomb for the pharaoh Khufu (Cheops in Greek), around 2560 BC. The pyramid was originally 481 feet tall, but today it is just 455 feet tall, as the tip has eroded over time. There are two smaller pyramids near the Great Pyramid of Giza — one built as a tomb for the pharaoh Khafre, and another built as a tomb for the pharaoh Menkaure.

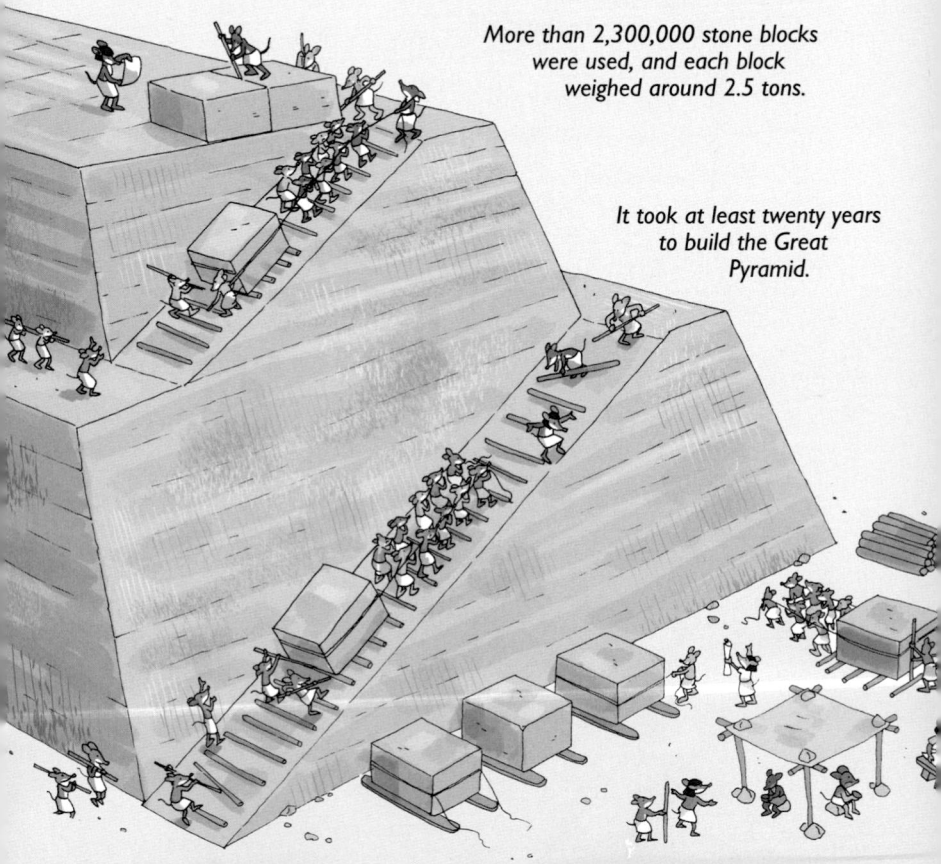

More than 2,300,000 stone blocks were used, and each block weighed around 2.5 tons.

It took at least twenty years to build the Great Pyramid.

It took at least 20,000–30,000 workers to build the Great Pyramid. These workers were not slaves; they were willing workers who often traveled from faraway villages. It was an honor to be part of the construction crew!

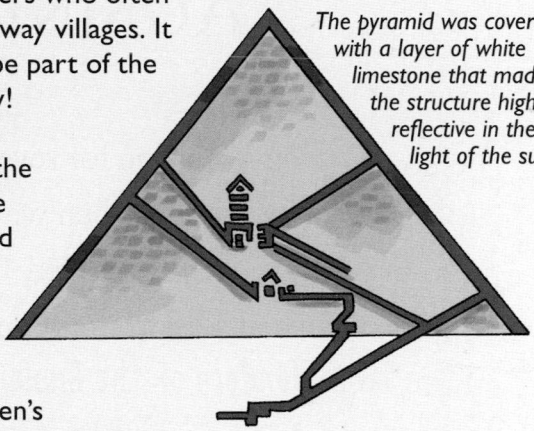

The pyramid was covered with a layer of white limestone that made the structure highly reflective in the light of the sun.

In the interior of the pyramid, there are both ascending and descending passageways as well as two rooms, the king's and the queen's chambers.

Many of the blocks that make up the pyramid are made of limestone, while other blocks are made of granite. It is generally believed that the Egyptians used copper or stone saws, chisels, and drills.

No one is entirely certain exactly how the Great Pyramid was constructed. Many believe workers pulled the stones up a series of ramps using special sleds. The workers most likely raised the large individual stone blocks into position using wooden and bronze levers.

On the Road Again!

We thanked Pyr-a-midion for revealing the ancient secrets of the pyramids. Then we said good-bye to him and Bab-beot and hurried back to our time machine. We had seen the only remaining wonder of the **Seven Wonders of the Ancient World**, and our visit to ancient Egypt had been a success!

"Now we're off to ancient Britain during the reign of King Arthur!" Professor von Volt announced once we had all climbed into the **Mouse Mover 3000**.

The little ship filled with a mysterious BLUE fog.

BANGGGGGGGGGGGGGGGGG!!!

My paws gripped the arms of the chair, and my head spun like a top.

The time machine began to vibrate, spinning faster and faster and faaaaaaassssssster!

THE SEVEN WONDERS OF THE ANCIENT WORLD

- Great Pyramid of Giza
- Statue of Zeus at Olympia
- Mausoleum at Halicarnassus
- Hanging Gardens of Babylon
- Colossus of Rhodes
- Lighthouse of Alexandria
- Temple of Artemis at Ephesus

A Castle on the Horizon

When we finally stopped moving, Professor von Volt opened the porthole cautiously.

"Look!" the professor exclaimed. "There's **CAMELOT CASTLE**!"

We climbed out of the Mouse Mover 3000 and gaped at the **ENORMOUSE** castle before us. Once again, the professor reached into his pocket and pulled out five teeny-tiny miniaturized costumes.

Professor von Volt used his secret potion to restore the clothes to their NORMAL size. I pulled on my brown tunic, green coat, striped tights, pointed shoes, leather satchel, and hat with a red feather. Then the professor handed us each five coins.

"I'll give each of you three copper coins, one SILVER coin, and one GOLD coin," he said. "The copper coins can buy you DINNER, the silver coin can buy you a **SWORD**, and the

MIDDLE AGES

THE LEGEND OF KING ARTHUR

No one is sure if King Arthur ever existed. Many historians today believe he is a fictitious character who is the stuff of folklore and legend. His story takes place during the Middle Ages (sometimes called the Medieval period) in European history. The Middle Ages lasted from the fifth until the fifteenth century.

gold coin can buy you a **HORSE**. Use them well!"

I put the coins in the leather satchel and slipped it across my chest.

We hid the **MOUSE MOVER 3000** behind a rock, covered it with moss, and headed toward the castle.

"We're now in **CAMELOT**, Britain, where, according to legend, the story of King Arthur and the Knights of the Round Table unfolded," Professor von Volt told us. "Our ***ADVENTURE*** is about to begin!"

Map of Great Britain

BRITANNIA
The word *Britannia* is Latin and is the ancient name for Great Britain. In the fifth century, Britannia was invaded by Saxon warriors from the northwestern part of modern-day Germany. According to legend, King Arthur led the British defense against the Saxons.

FIFTH CENTURY OR THE TWELFTH CENTURY?
Although King Arthur is believed to have ruled during the fifth century, the most well-known tales of his exploits were written during the twelfth century. These poets and writers used twelfth-century descriptions of scenery and costumes in their work, which is what you'll see depicted here.

Caerleon
BRITANNIA
Avalon
Tintagel
Stonehenge
Camelot
BRITTANY
Brocéliande
(Paimpont forest)

AVALON: The magical island where King Arthur's sword Excalibur was forged and where some believe King Arthur was buried.

CAMELOT: The castle where King Arthur and his court lived.

CAERLEON: City on the Usk River in modern-day Wales that is associated with King Arthur's legendary Round Table.

TINTAGEL CASTLE: King Arthur's birthplace.

BROCÉLIANDE: A legendary forest in the rough location of modern-day Paimpont forest, in Brittany, France, where Merlin's tomb is said to be found.

STONEHENGE: A prehistoric monument of enormous stones built sometime between 3000 and 2000 BC.

Excerpt from the poem

"Idylls of the King"

by Alfred, Lord Tennyson

. . . Then rose the King and
moved his host by night,
And ever pushed Sir Modred,
league by league,
Back to the sunset bound
of Lyonnesse —
A land of old upheaven
from the abyss
By fire, to sink into the abyss again;
Where fragments of forgotten
peoples dwelt,
And the long mountains
ended in a coast
Of ever-shifting sand, and far away
The phantom circle of
a moaning sea . . .

Feudal lord or king

Vassal

Lords

Villeins

Serfs

FEUDALISM

Feudalism was a type of government during medieval times. The **feudal lord** or **king** gave a large estate (called a **fief**) to a **vassal**. In exchange for the land, the vassal agreed to be loyal to the king. The **vassal** would then divide up the land further and give it to his **lords**, who agreed to provide knights who would fight for the king. The lord gave land to the **villeins**, who had to farm the land for the lord. At the very bottom were the **serfs**. They had no land and were considered to be the property of the lord.

CAMELOT? THIS ISN'T CAMELOT!

By the time we reached the castle, the sun had set. The castle was surrounded by a very **deep** moat, and the drawbridge was raised. The flag flying in front of the castle had an image of a flea on it. *How odd!*

"Let's pretend to be a troupe of ACTORS," Professor von Volt suggested. "That way we'll blend in."

Then he shouted toward the castle: "Hello, citizens of **Camelot**!"

A tiny window opened, and a snout appeared.

"Who is it? Who goes there?" the sentry asked. "What does Camelot have to do with anything? This is FLEA FLICKER CASTLE!"

"Whaaaaat?" the professor whispered to us.

"We came to the wrong place. How odd!"

"Open the gate! We're actors!" Trap shouted back.

"How do I know you're telling the **truth**?" the sentry asked suspiciously.

Trap began juggling several **COLORED** balls in the air. **POP! POP! POP!** He managed to catch each one and send it into the air again.

"See?" Trap said. "And my oldest friend here plays the flute, the maiden **sings**, and the little one is a jester."

The sentry pointed to me.

"What about the one with the butterflies on his nose?" he asked.

Butterflies? He must

MIDDLE AGES

EYEGLASSES

Eyeglasses were invented in the thirteenth century in Italy. The monk Alessandro della Spina was the first person to produce them for others. There were many other things that hadn't been invented yet during the Middle Ages, like postage stamps and modern toilets. People used chamber pots instead!

have been talking about my **glasses**.

"I — ahem," I said, taking a step forward, "I'm a minstrel!"

"Really?" the sentry asked. "Then recite a poem!"

Holey cheese! My mind went **BLANK**. I couldn't come up with anything!

"Think of something, quick!" Trap whispered as he pinched my tail.

So I improvised:

In the evenings, traveling minstrels entertained citizens with songs that told of courageous heroes, wars, and love.

"Oh, mouse in the castle
Please let us come in,
Our show is so cheesy
You'll laugh and you'll grin!
Our music and jokes
Are better than the rest,
And my rhymes, you can see,
Are simply the best!"

The sentry shook his head.

"Bah, there's nothing special about that poem, but I'll let you come in anyway," he said. "We're bored. There's nothing to do here. Even if your show stinks, it will still be entertaining!"

With a creak, the drawbridge came down. A short, one-eyed mouse with ruffled whiskers came to meet us.

"Follow me," he said. "I'm Cyclops McMouse."

As we followed him through the courtyard, I looked around me. In one corner, a blacksmith was forging a horseshoe on an anvil. Nearby, a farmer loaded hay on a cart. The baker was taking crispy loaves of rye bread out of an oven while an apprentice was weaving on a loom inside the tailor's shop.

My maiden!
Toot-toot-
toot-toot!
Oh, my hero!

MIDDLE AGES

CASTLES

Castles had no running water or sewers. The windows were very small and didn't have glass. Curtained canopies hung around the beds and were closed at night to keep in the heat.

Cyclops McMouse took us through a maze of **passageways** until we came to a vast hall paved with **BLACK** and **WHITE** stones. Small torches on the walls cast an **EERIE** glow. There was a glowing **fireplace** at the other end of the hall, but the space was so enormouse that our side of the room was freezing **cold**. Here and there hung embroidered **tapestries** depicting great medieval scenes.

Cyclops McMouse lowered his voice.

"Be careful what you say," he warned. "Sir Flea Flicker isn't a very trusting **mouse**. If he doesn't like the looks of you, he'll chop off your head!"

I was **worried**.

1
2
3
4
5
6
7
8
9
10
11
12
13
14

INSIDE THE CASTLE

1. Castle's banner
2. Tower
3. Battlements
4. Arrow slit
5. Drawbridge
6. Moat filled with water
7. Knight
8. Dungeon where prisoners are kept
9. Mechanism to lift the drawbridge
10. Treasury
11. Armor
12. Banquet hall
13. Bedroom
14. Roof
15. Armory
16. Coronation room
17. Sentry
18. Archer
19. Thick brick walls
20. Secret passage
21. Kitchen
22. Pantry

"His son, Flea Flicker Junior, is the same way," Cyclops continued. "He loves to see heads **roll**."

"Oh, I'm not worried," Trap said confidently. "Leave it to me. I'll entertain them with my most **INCREDIBLE** jokes, like this one: What do you call a mosquito in a tin suit? A bite in shining armor! Ha, ha, ha, ha!"

At the end of the hall, I saw a very **LOOONG** table covered with food. Knights were sitting and talking and eating. Some were playing **CHESS**. In a corner, the ladies were busy embroidering as they talked and talked. Sir Flea Flicker, the lord of the castle, was short and stocky with a stubby nose and disheveled fur. He wore a **LOOONG** purple velvet cloak embroidered with little golden fleas that was **stained** with greasy spots.

At his right was his son, Flea Flicker Junior, a big mouse with **greasy** fur, mangy whiskers, and **crooked yellow** teeth.

MIDDLE AGES

HYGIENE

The rich bathed in wooden tubs filled with warm water and used soap made from ashes and sheep's fat. To cover their body odor between baths, they used perfume.

Cyclops bowed until his whiskers touched the ground.

"Oh, noble sir," he announced loudly. "A troupe of actors has come with the hopes of enlivening this **somber** night!"

I peeked at Sir Flea Flicker to see what effect this introduction might have had. He scratched himself. **Scratch, scratch, scratch!** Then he squashed a flea. **Squish!**

"Humpf!" Sir Flea Flicker mumbled. "If they don't entertain me, **CHOP OFF THEIR HEADS**!"

"Right!" Cyclops McMouse agreed. "If they don't entertain us, **chop, chop**!"

All the knights shouted at the same time: **"Chop, chop, chop!"**

SAY SOMETHING POETIC!

A rat wearing a **BLACK** hood stepped forward.

"There's someone to **decapitate**, huh?" he asked gruffly. "I want to test my new ax!"

He tore out one of his whiskers, tossed it in the air, and cut it with his ax. **CHOP!**

Even Trap looked worried now.

"Cousin, say something **poetic**, or they'll chop off our heads!" he whispered as he **PINCHED** my tail.

"Don't rush me!" I squeaked. "I can't think when I'm under **PRESSURE**!"

I didn't know what else to say,

Sir Flea Flicker's henchmouse

so I tried to flatter the mean, scruffy Sir Flea Flicker:

"Oh, Sir Flea Flicker,
So noble and wise,
We're so glad to meet you,
And all of your guys.
Your castle is mighty,
Your knights are quite brave,
And the cheese that you serve,
The locals all crave!"

"Humpf!" Sir Flea Flicker replied. "Not bad. I didn't know my cheese was so POPULAR."

I breathed a sigh of relief. We were **saved**!

But then he looked at Trap, Thea, the professor, and Benjamin.

"What about these four?" he asked suspiciously. "What can they do?"

Trap began telling joke after joke after joke.

MEDIEVAL LAUGHS

Q: *Why did the king go to the dentist?*
A: *To get his teeth crowned.*

A knight goes to a shoemaker.
"I would like a pair of boots," he says.
"What color, sir?"
"Both the same, please!"

The lord of the castle meets a friend who lives in a nearby castle.
"Dear friend, can you lend me one hundred pieces of gold?" he asks.
"Oh, I have only one silver coin in my pocket," the friend replies.
"And at the castle?" the lord asks.
"Everyone's fine at the castle, thank you!"

Q: *What king of medieval England was famous because he spent so many nights at his Round Table writing books?*
A: *King Author!*

A knight meets a friend.

"Hello, Sir Mousey," he says. "You've changed so much! You're much thinner than you used to be, your fur is much longer, and your whiskers are blond instead of black."

"My name isn't Sir Mousey," the other knight replies.

The first knight is shocked. "You even changed your name!"

A knight writes to his loved one.

"Fair maiden, I'd cross a thousand enchanted forests to see you again! I'd face a thousand enemy soldiers! I'd fight a thousand ferocious dragons!"

"Well then, come see me now!" the maiden writes back.

"Now?" the knight writes back. "But it's raining!"

"Tomorrow is my wife's birthday, and I don't know what to get her," one knight tells another.

"Give her a pretty silk handkerchief," the other knight answers.

"Hmmm," the first knight replies. "But I don't know the size of her nose!"

A Food Fight . . . with Pie!

Professor von Volt began to play a merry melody, Thea sang, and Benjamin danced a little jig.

Danced a little jig... Danced a little jig... Danced a little jig... Danced a little jig...

A procession of servants entered the hall carrying **pewter** dishes of meat, chestnut fritters, quince jelly, blueberry jam, dried figs, and raisins.

Last in line was a TINY servant around Benjamin's age. He was struggling to carry an **ENORMOUSE** pie that was decorated with a **tiny** flag bearing the Flea Flicker Castle emblem.

As the tiny servant made his way to the table, he tripped on one of the knights' swords and fell. The pie ended up on Sir Flea Flicker's **face**. The lord's snout turned bright red with embarrassment.

"**Get that mouse!**" he shouted.

To save the little mouselet, Trap grabbed three

apples and began juggling them in the air. He was trying to distract Sir Flea Flicker! Trap jumped up on a table. He balanced a spoon on the tip of his snout and spun a pewter dish on top of the spoon. Meanwhile, he continued juggling the apples while his tail waved the little flag that had been in the pie.

Everyone in the court was AMAZED.

"Hurrah!" they cheered loudly.

Trap put down all of his props. As his grand FINALE, he took a piece of pie and threw it in the nearest knight's face.

I held my breath, waiting to see how Sir Flea Flicker would react. But after a moment of shock, he laughed so hard he almost choked. Then he began throwing pieces of pie at his guests. It was a food fight . . . with pie! Everyone burst out laughing.

Hee, hee, hee!

Ha, ha, ha!

Ho, ho ho!

I sighed with relief. The little servant was safe! While the food fight continued, I approached the trembling mouselet. He was as PALE as a slice of mozzarella!

"Everything's fine, little one," I reassured him. "Don't be afraid. What's your name?"

"**Crouton**, sir," he replied softly. "I'm an orphan. I don't have a mother or father."

As we were talking, a messenger sounded three blasts on a trumpet and handed Sir Flea Flicker a piece of **parchment**.

Toot-toot-toot! Toot-toot-toot!

The trumpeter sounded again:

Toot-toot-toot! Toot-toot-tooooot!

MIDDLE AGES

AT THE TABLE

People ate porridge and other hot cereals, vegetables, black bread, eggs, and wild meat and game caught in the forest. Knives were used to cut the meat, which was then eaten using one's fingers instead of a fork!

Hurrah!
Hurrah!

Grunt!
Double grunt!

"Stop tooting in my ear!" Sir Flea Flicker shouted. "Oof!"

Then he read the parchment.

"Oh, son, get ready!" he shouted with **EXCITEMENT**. "All of Britannia's knights are on their way here, to Flea Flicker Castle. A grand tournament will be held, and the winner will become the **new king**!"

"Papa, are you saying I'll be the next king?" Flea Flicker Junior shouted. "Huh? Huh? Huh?"

THE IMPOSSIBLE CHALLENGE

Sir Flea Flicker sniffed the air. **sniff! sniff!**

"What's that nice smell?" he asked.

Trap bowed down until his WHISKERS touched the floor. Then he removed a Gorgonzola cheese sandwich from his satchel.

"It's **GORGONZOLA CHEESE**, my sire!" he said. "Would you like to taste it?"

Sir Flea Flicker's personal taster

Sir Flea Flicker gestured to a mouse standing nearby. The **fat** little rodent took the sandwich, smelled it **cautiously**, and then took a little bite.

During the Middle Ages, many lords used powerful poisons to kill their rivals. That's why many lords had their own personal tasters. It was that person's duty to try foods before they were given to the lord to make sure they weren't poisoned.

It is generally believed that John Montagu, fourth earl of Sandwich, invented the sandwich sometime in the late 1700s. According to legend, he frequently asked to be served slices of meat between two pieces of bread so that he didn't have to interrupt his card games to eat a formal meal.

Little **Crouton** leaned toward me.

"That's Sir Flea Flicker's new personal TASTER!" he whispered. "Three have died in the last month."

"So can I eat it?" Sir Flea Flicker asked eagerly.

"It's **delicious**, my lord," he said.

"I know it's good," Sir Flea Flicker replied impatiently. "I can smell it! But how do you **feel**?"

"I feel great, sire!" He licked his whiskers.

He tried to take another bite, but Sir Flea Flicker grabbed the sandwich.

"MEDIEVAL MOZZARELLA!" he shouted. "You're supposed to **TASTE** it, not **eat** it. There'll be nothing left for me!"

Sir Flea Flicker bit into the sandwich and ate the whole thing in just three bites.

"That's quite an appetite!" exclaimed Trap.

Sir Flea Flicker wiped his mouth on his sleeve and let out a belch. **BURP!**

"Hey, you," Sir Flea Flicker said, pointing at Trap. "I nominate you to be the castle's new **COOK**! Prepare a pot of this GORGONSOMETHING-OR-OTHER. I want to look good when the knights come to dine here next week. Make it **delicious**, or off with your head. *CHOP!*"

Trap snapped to attention.

"Got it, chief!" Trap replied. "There'll be **Gorgonzola** cheese for the knights that will be whisker-licking good!"

A round rat with curly fur elbowed his way in.

"But **I'm** the castle cook!" he protested, wielding a wooden spoon.

"Oh, come on!" my cousin squeaked. "I'm better than you! I know a whole **BUNCH** of things you don't!"

"Really?" the cook challenged him. "Name a food, and I'll cook it — I give you my word!"

"Okay, fine!" Trap replied, a smug look on his snout. "Make me a glass of orange juice."

"Hmmm, orange juice?" the rat replied. "Pardon me, but what is that?"

"Okay, make me TOMATO SAUCE," Trap said.

"Hmmm, tomato?" the rat replied. "MEDIEVAL MOZZARELLA, what is that?"

"Well, then, I'd love a slice of pineapple!" Trap replied triumphantly.

"Pineapple? Never heard of it!"

"I bet you that you don't even know how to bake

After the year 1492, a lot of new foods were introduced to Europeans from America. New animals that had been almost entirely unknown to Europeans, such as the modern-day parrot, were also imported from the New World.

a **chocolate** cake, do you?" Trap taunted. "Or make a cup of **COFFEE**?"

"**Chocolate**? **COFFEE**?" the cook sobbed. "Never heard of them. That's it! You **won**. You're the better cook!"

Benjamin **CHUCKLED**.

"I told Uncle Trap that tomatoes, pineapples, and chocolate were imported to Europe from **America** after 1492," he told me. "Coffee came from the **Middle East** and the orange came from **CHINA**. That's why no one here in the Middle Ages knows what these foods are yet!"

BRING ME THE GORGONZOLA!

Sir Flea Flicker granted Trap everything he needed to make the Gorgonzola cheese dinner, and he gave Trap permission to go **anywhere** in the castle he wanted.

"Yay!" Benjamin cheered. "This will give us a chance to **explore** the entire castle!"

We chatted with guards, artisans, and farmers, but no one had ever heard of **Camelot** or **KING ARTHUR**.

"It's very odd that the **CHRONOMETER** didn't take us to Camelot!" Professor von Volt said.

Trap was busy mass-producing Gorgonzola cheese. He used milk in **HUGE** oak barrels that had been rolled into the castle's courtyard from nearby **farms**. It would be a few days until

the cheese was **ready**.

We knew the cheese was ready by the **stinky** smell. Sir Flea Flicker descended on the kitchen, **GREEDILY** sniffing the air.

"BRING ME THE GORGONZOLA!"

Trap spread Gorgonzola on some toast. He garnished it with an olive that looked like a **flea**.

"Ta-da!" Trap exclaimed. "FLEA FLICKER CASTLE'S STINKY TOASTED BREAD!"

The taster barely had time to take a **nibble** and give the okay before Sir Flea Flicker gobbled it up. After he was done, Sir Flea Flicker **dove** into the caldron to eat some more.

"Yummy, yum, yum!" he cried as he came up for air. He was covered in cheese from the tips of his **whiskers** to the end of his **tail**. "Soon all of Britannia's knights will taste and envy my Gorgonzola!"

MERLIN'S EYES

I was sleeping on a straw mat in a corner of the kitchen the next morning near Trap, Thea, Benjamin, and the professor when I woke with a start. The first **rays of the sun** filtered in through a small window, and an imposing figure stood before me. He wore a blue cloak and a tall conical hat with **gold** stars embroidered on it. An owl flew in the window and came to rest on his shoulder with a gentle **rustle**. He smoothed his long white beard and looked at us with **PENETRATING** blue eyes.

"I am Merlin," he **GREETED** us. "What

MIDDLE AGES

MERLIN

According to legend, Merlin was King Arthur's advisor. He was in love with the beautiful young Niviane. He revealed to her all his magical secrets, but she took advantage of that knowledge and locked him in a magical prison, where he perished.

are your **names**? Are you travelers? I have heard that you have **incredible** magical abilities."

Professor von Volt **BOWED** respectfully.

"So good to meet you, wise Merlin," he replied. "Yes, we are travelers. We come from **FAR, FAR** away."

"I feel that is so," Merlin replied with a nod. "You come from a country outside of reality — unreachable even to me. . . ."

A **SHADOW** passed over his eyes.

"Well, travelers who come from a faraway place, I will tell you a secret," he continued. "In this castle, there is a treasure more precious than **silver** or **gold**. That is why I am here — to reveal the **hidden** treasure so that Britannia can reach its full potential!"

At that moment, a ray of **sunlight** shined directly into my eyes, temporarily blinding me. I rubbed my eyes. When I opened them again, the wizard had **DISAPPEARED**!

Had I been **DREAMING**?

"Geronimo, there's a treasure here!" Trap exclaimed. "Let's go find it!"

I guess I was **awake** after all!

"What do you say, Geronimo?" Trap continued. "Even a teeny-tiny treasure would be enough to make this trip worthwhile. Let's **GO**!"

Suddenly, we heard the sound of the trumpet.

Toot-toot-toot-tooooooooot!

"Make way for the **bravest** knights in Britanniaaaaaaaa! Make waaaaaay!"

We glanced out the window.

MIDDLE AGES

CLOTHES

Farmers and other average citizens wore cloth shirts, trousers, leggings, and cloaks. The lords wore embroidered wool or silk clothing dyed bright colors. They were embroidered and decorated with gold, silver, pearls, and precious stones. The lords' clothes were so valuable that they were left to their children as part of their inheritance.

Sure enough, a thick cloud of **dust** covered the road leading to Flea Flicker Castle. Hundreds — no, THOUSANDS — of knights were galloping toward the castle. Each knight carried a **multicolored** banner that waved briskly in the wind. It was an **extraordinary** sight!

Thea quickly snapped a photo. I took out my travel journal and jotted down a few thoughts:

The knights who are to challenge one another for the crown of the King of Britannia are arriving!

"Hurry up, Geronimo," Trap said. "Stop **daydreaming** and help me wash the dishes!"

A Mouselet with Golden Braids

Once I finished washing the dishes, I went to the courtyard to throw out the garbage.

On my way back into the kitchen, I saw a tiny mouselet with **LONG** blonde braids and a light blue tunic. She wore a silver pendant in the shape of a **heart** with the letter **G** engraved on it.

"That's KING LEODEGRANCE of Carmelide's daughter," I heard someone whisper.

I watched as the little princess strolled toward the stream next to the castle. She went up the **STONE** bridge that crossed the stream. Then she leaned over to watch the ***rushing*** water below. The knot that held the pendant **loosened**.

The little mouselet tried to grab the necklace, but it fell down into the stream.

Crouton was nearby. Without a hint of hesitation, he jumped into the **frigid** water. A few seconds later, he emerged, holding the pendant. With a bow, he held it out to the mouselet.

"Thank you!" she said, tears of **JOY** in her eyes. "This piece of jewelry is the only remembrance I have of my mother!"

"I understand," Crouton whispered shyly. "I don't have a father or mother."

The two smiled, and I immediately knew they had become friends.

I ran to Crouton and wrapped him in my coat. Even so, his teeth continued to CHATTER.

"Come into the kitchen and warm up by the FIRE, little one," I urged him. He waved good-bye to the golden-haired mouselet, and we went back inside the castle.

For My Cousin, That's Nothing!

The next morning I woke to hear the sound of someone sobbing in the courtyard outside the kitchen window. I woke my cousin Trap and **dragged** him outside with me.

"Why'd you have to wake me, Geronimo? **Huh? Huh?**" Trap whined. "I was in the middle of the most **incredible** dream! I had just located the treasure hidden in the castle, and I was **RICH, RICH, RICH**!"

"Shhh!" I shushed my cousin, pointing to a sobbing old rodent leaning against a tree. "That mouse is very **UPSET**. Let's see if we can help.

"Excuse me, sir," I said. "Is everything okay?"

"Oh, my poor, darling Mousilda!" the old rodent sobbed. "I'd save her myself, but alas, I

am too **old**! *Brrrrrrrgh!*"

He blew his nose on his coat sleeve.

"I don't understand . . ." I began. Someone tugged **gently** on my tail. It was Crouton!

"Psst, Geronimo," he whispered. "That's Sir Ratford of Cheddarshire. His daughter, Mousilda, is being held **PRISONER** in the tallest tower of the super-scary **BLACK CASTLE**!"

How terrible! I had to do something to help.

"Sir Ratford, my name is Stilton, *Geronimo Stilton*," I told the sad rodent. "I will save your daughter!"

"You will?" he exclaimed, overcome with **joy**. "Thank you, most noble rodent. Thank you!"

He hugged me **TIGHTLY**. My snout turned **PURPLE** with embarrassment.

Crouton tugged my tail again.

"Sir Geronimo," he whispered, "are you sure you want to do this? No other knight has dared to enter the BLACK CASTLE."

"Of course he dares to save Mousilda!" Trap exclaimed. "My cousin is a very brave mouse."

I was? No, no, no! I'm not a brave mouse at all! In fact, I'm very, very scared. Back home in New Mouse City, I'm known for being the biggest scaredy-mouse. But if someone needed my help, I couldn't say no.

"But there are strange legends about the BLACK CASTLE," Crouton continued. "They say there are gigantic leeches in the moat. . . ."

"Pff, for my cousin, that's nothing!" Trap replied.

"They say there's a fire-breathing dragon in the courtyard. . . ."

"Pff, for my cousin, that's nothing!" Trap replied.

The Black Castle

"They say that the Black Knight dumps **boiling hot fondue** on whoever tries to get in. . . ."

"Pff, for my cousin, that's nothing!" Trap replied.

Gigantic leeches? A fire-breathing dragon?? Boiling hot fondue???

Gigantic leeches

Why, why, oh, why had I agreed to come on this wacky journey through time?

Fire-breathing dragon

A moment later, an enormouse rat in black armor with a face that would scare even a **RABID** cat came galloping up to Flea Flicker Castle on his horse. His coat of arms was a **prancing** black rat with a **forked** tail.

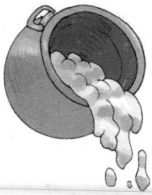

Boiling hot fondue

"I am Winston Wickedpaw, from the noble house of Drake Mudrat, also known as the **Black Knight**. I hear that someone here has challenged the great Drake Mudrat!"

Boy, word sure did travel **quickly** in the Middle Ages!

"That's right!" Trap replied boldly. "My cousin *Geronimo Stilton* is going to save the maiden Mousilda."

"Oh, really?" Winston Wickedpaw asked. He turned to me and pointed his super-pointy lance at my snout. "I dare you — no, I **double** dare you to, you measly little mouse!"

"He accepts your challenge!" Trap replied **BOLDLY**. "Make ready your whiskers, **Winston Wickedpaw**. My cousin Geronimo Stilton will follow you to the **BLACK CASTLE**, where he will defeat **Drake Mudrat** and save the maiden Mousilda! Isn't that right, Geronimo?"

Trap pulled my ear.

"Don't you wimp out now, **scaredy-mouse**!" he whispered.

WINSTON WICKEDPAW shook his fist at me.

"I'll wait for you at the **BLACK CASTLE**, Geronimo of Stilton!" he said. "Ooooooh, you're in big trouble! Drake Mudrat is one seriously scary mouse!"

I turned as **PALE** as a slice of mozzarella. A moment later, I fainted!

BOILING HOT FONDUE SHAMPOO

When I came to, I was wearing a suit of **armor**. Sir Ratford of Cheddarshire and his squires had already dressed me!

"Bring him a horse!" Sir Ratford shouted.

"Yes, of course, bring me a horse," I said. "Wait, what? A horse? I don't know how to ride a horse!"

But Sir Ratford and his squires used a pulley to haul me onto the horse. Then I headed at a gallop toward the **BLACK CASTLE**.

Medieval armor began as chain mail, made of small metal rings linked together. This developed into the more protective plate mail, made of metal plates covering the body along with a metal helmet. Shields were made from wooden planks that were covered in leather and painted.

Here's the shield!
Creak!
Creak!
Creak!
Why me?
Heave, ho!
Pull!
Let go!
Push!

MIDDLE AGES

FORESTS

In the Middle Ages, forests were much more expansive than they are today. Wild animals like bears and wolves lived among the trees along with hermits and bandits.

Actually, the horse galloped while I hung on to the saddle for **dear life**! On the way to the **BLACK CASTLE**, I fell off the horse three times! After the third fall, I decided to walk the rest of the way.

It was hard to move through the forest with the armor and sword, so I left them behind. I arrived at the **BLACK CASTLE** at the top of **Black Hill** in the middle of **Black Forest** at night. The creek that ran alongside the castle was **black**. The walls of the castle were **black**, the roof was **black**, the door was **black**, and the banner that flapped on the highest tower was **black**. The cawing crows that gloomily circled the castle's towers were **black**, too.

Caw, caw, caaaaaaaawwwwww!

Before I got any nearer, I took a deep breath to calm my nerves.

I glanced worriedly at the moat, but I didn't see any leeches. So I straightened up, gathered all my COURAGE, and approached the castle.

"Er, is anyone there?" I shouted at the massive **black** door.

A pair of whiskers peered down at me from the top of a tall tower.

"Who goes there?" the guard asked.

"Ahem — I'm the carpenter," I replied. "Someone sent a message about a BROKEN LADDER."

MIDDLE AGES

SIEGE

If a castle was about to be attacked, sentinels sounded the alarm, and the drawbridge was raised. Archers shot arrows through the castle wall's arrowslits. Meanwhile, the enemy attacked with fiery arrows, rams, mobile towers, and catapults. Sieges could last for months because castles kept a large stock of supplies.

"In this castle, there's always something **rotting** away," he **grumbled**. "Even the roof is falling apart!

"I'm waiting for a **knight**, a certain Geronimo of Stilton," he continued as I followed him inside. "My orders are to drop a caldron of **boiling hot fondue** on his head! Lucky for you, you identified yourself!"

"Lucky me!" I agreed, breathing a secret sigh of **RELIEF**. "I've heard there are some pretty bloodthirsty leeches in the moat. And that fire-breathing dragon must keep things **toasty** warm in the winter!"

The guard chuckled.

Catapult (to hurl stones at the enemy)

"I shouldn't be telling you this because it's a secret, but that rumor about the leeches is just made up to keep **gawkers** away," he said. "And it works, too! No one dares to get anywhere near the castle! Besides, if anyone does come near, I take care of them with a shampoo of **boiling hot fondue**!"

I laughed through gritted teeth.

"Ha, ha, ha," I said. **"Funny!"**

As soon as I could, I slipped away through a **DARK** hallway and went up the stairs that took me to the highest tower.

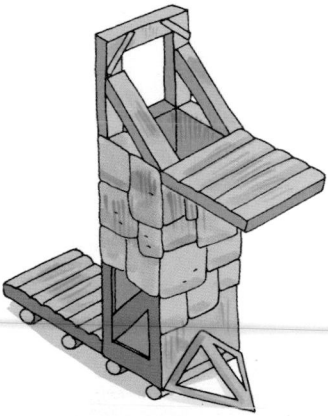

Mobile tower (used to climb up the wall)

Ram (used to break down the walls and doors)

OH, I'M SO AFRAID OF HEIGHTS!

I climbed and climbed and climbed. Ugh! Those stairs seemed to go on **FOREVER**!

I got to the tippy-top of the tower and saw a teensy-weensy little **black** door with the Black Knight's coat of arms above it. A thick, rusted key was stuck in the door. I turned it and the little door **SCREECHED** open.

"Do not be afraid, maiden Mousilda!" I cried. "I am here to **save** you!"

I looked around the **black** room. There was a canopied bed with brocaded **black** curtains. Next to the **black** stone fireplace, a melancholy little mouselet with fur as white as snow was busy knitting.

She was dressed in a **GOLD** silk gown and wore a crown studded with rubies. She jumped up.

"Who are you, brave knight?" she squeaked.

I bowed.

"My name is Stilton, *Geronimo Stilton*," I replied. "I'm here to save you!"

I heard the **thud** of heavy footsteps coming up the stairs, and I saw the light of a torch project a dark shadow on the floor. It was **Drake Mudrat**!

We quickly hid behind some armor.

"Mousilda, **WHERE** are you hiding?" Drake Mudrat asked in a SINGSONG voice. "Don't you want to marry me, **little mouse of my heart**?"

He peeked behind the brocaded **black** curtains. While he was

distracted, Mousilda and I **SLIPPED** out the door and began descending the stairs on tiptoe.

Suddenly, I caught a whiff of stinky garlic.

Achoo! I sneezed loudly.

Drake Mudrat turned. His garlicky breath was making me sneeze uncontrollably!

Achoo, achoo, achoo!

Why, why, oh, why did I have to be allergic to garlic?

"So you've come!" Drake Mudrat shouted as he chased us down the stairs. "I'll catch you, Geronimo of Stilton, and I'll pluck out all your whiskers!"

I heard a clatter from below: **SOLDIERS**!

Our only hope was to ESCAPE through a tiny window and get to the roof of the castle. Once we were on the roof, I made the mistake of looking down.

Medieval mozzarella! I'm so afraid of heights!

We were up really, really HIGH!

I grabbed Mousilda's paw and, carefully trying to keep our balance, we made our way onto the battlements. Beneath us the archers aimed their arrows at us. They flew past us. One GRAZED my ear, another PIERCED the feather of my hat, while a third arrow sliced off one of my whiskers!

Mousilda was wearing a long dress that hampered our progress, so I carried her in my arms and ran as fast as I could while I tried not to look down.

I'm afraid of heights, I'm afraid of heights, I'm afraid of heights, I'm afraid of heights, I'm afraid of heights, I'm afraid of heights, I'm afraid

Crack!

I had almost reached the stairs leading to the courtyard when I slipped on a pile of **CROW DROPPINGS**!

Caw!

Mousilda and I rolled down the roof. Luckily, I grabbed the embankment as we went over the edge. A second later, we were **dangling** high above the ground.

"**HEEEEEEEEEEEELP!**" we screamed. "Please help us!"

Right below us in the courtyard, I saw four **familiar** faces. It was Professor von Volt, Thea, Trap, and Benjamin.

"Hang on, Uncle!" Benjamin shouted.

The four of them scampered up the stairs, and seconds later, they had grabbed us and pulled us to **SAFETY**.

MOZZARELLA PERFUME

"Phew! This time I was sure I was a goner." I sighed. "I thought I would lose my fur!"

We ran **DOWN** the stairs, **CROSSED** the courtyard, and hurried over the drawbridge just as it was beginning to rise. Then we hopped on our horses and **GALLOPED** back toward Flea Flicker Castle.

Mousilda didn't fall off her horse once. Can you guess how many times I fell? **THIRTEEN!** I bruised both **ears**, my right **knee**, my left big **toe**, three **whiskers**, the tip of my **nose**, my left **pinky**, my **tail**, my right **wrist**, my left **incisor** . . . and my **bottom**!

When we finally got back to Flea Flicker Castle, I slid to the floor, **EXHAUSTED**.

Sir Ratford hugged me, tears in his eyes.

"Ask me for anything, anything, absolutely anything you want!" he told me. "Do you want **land**, or a **castle**, or **riches**?"

"Oh, ask for a chest full of **gold**!" Trap whispered excitedly. "Or a coffer full of **PEARLS**!"

"There is no need to give me anything!" I told Sir Ratford.

Sir Ratford took his sword and solemnly laid it first on my **left** shoulder, and then on my **right**.

"Geronimo of Stilton, I name you **KNIGHT**!" he said. "Do you promise to defend the **WEAK** and mend the **injustices** in the world?"

"I promise!" I agreed proudly.

"**HOORAY!**" everyone cheered. "Hip, hip, hooray! Three cheers for Geronimo of Stilton!"

"Well done, Uncle!" Benjamin said sweetly.

I heard a **CLICK** and knew my sister was busy snapping photos.

Click!
Well done, Uncle!

MIDDLE AGES

KNIGHTS

Knights had to respect and obey the Code of Chivalry. The code was a set of rules of honor, and included promises to fight for the welfare of all, to protect the weak, to live by honor and for glory, and to always keep one's word.

"Where are you from, my **BRaVe** knight?" Mousilda asked.

"I am from far, far away," I told her. "I will be leaving soon."

"Will you return to Flea Flicker Castle?" she asked.

"**WHO KNOWS?**" I replied. "I may be back some day!"

"Well, then, Sir Geronimo, however far you travel, know that I will always keep the memory of your generous gesture in my **HeaRt**," she said. "And here's something to help you remember me."

She handed me a white handkerchief that had the *delicate* scent of mozzarella perfume.

I accepted the handkerchief.

"Thank you," I replied humbly. "It would be impossible to forget you, my lady!"

THE GOLD ARROW

The following morning we heard the sound of a trumpet: It was the beginning of the tournament to crown the king of Britannia!

Toot-toot-toot! Toot-toot-toot!
Toot-toot-toot!
Tooooooooooooot!

"The tournament will begin with the **archery** competition," the herald announced. "The most valiant shooters will compete for the prize of the **GOLD ARROW**!"

The contestants shot one arrow after another.

When it was **Flea Flicker Junior's** turn, he took aim.

"Now I'll show you how it's done!" he shouted.

He shot three arrows one after another, all

within the target, and closer to the center than anyone else's arrows.

The crowd cheered:

"FLEA FLICKER JUNIOR!
FLEA FLICKER JUNIOR!
FLEA FLICKER JUNIOR!"

He preened himself.

"Yes, I'm good, and I know it!" he said.

The herald made an announcement: "The winner of the contest is —"

But a voice interrupted him.

"I want to try, too!" came the mouse's squeak.

The contestant came forward, her face covered by the brim of her hat. But I recognized her immediately. It was my sister, **Thea**!

She pushed her hat down so no one would recognize her. Then she notched the arrow and prepared to shoot. My whiskers trembled with excitement!

Thea squinted, took aim, and released the arrow. It whistled through the air.

Tournaments took place either on foot or on horses, and knights competed alone or in teams. These spectacular events were originally intended as training for war. Eventually, they became performances for members of the court.

SWISHHHHHHHHHHHHHHHH!

It hit the **BULL'S-EYE**!

She released another arrow: **BULL'S-EYE**!

She shot again: **BULL'S-EYE**!

Thea took off her hat, and everyone recognized her.

bull's-eye

Flea Flicker Junior was **purple** with anger.

"I can't believe she beat me!" he shouted.

"Wow, she's **GOOD**. . . ." the crowd murmured. "She rocks! She's way better than Flea Flicker Junior!"

Thea **accepted** the Gold Arrow as her prize as Trap, Benjamin, Professor von Volt, and I chanted: *"Nothing can stop the Stilton family!"*

MIDDLE AGES

WOMEN

Women did not have the same rights as men during the Middle Ages. Women could not choose their own husbands or inherit land, and they had to obey their fathers and husbands. Still, there were many valiant female figures during the Middle Ages, such as the nun Hildegard of Bingen (1098–1179), a writer, composer, and philosopher; powerful Queen Eleanor of Aquitaine (1122–1204); and the heroic Joan of Arc (1412–1431), who led the French to important war victories.

HEAR YE, HEAR YE, HEAR YE!

At noon, the herald made another announcement:

"Hear ye, hear ye, hear ye! The Grand Rat of Rattonia will **CHALLENGE** Measly Marvin of Mousehampton to a duel."

Two knights came riding into the arena on their steeds. They stopped and waited as their horses pawed **nervously** at the ground. The starting signal sounded, and the knights grabbed their **LONG** lances and galloped toward each other.

The two knights clashed with a **metallic** sound: **Claaaaank!** High in the stands, I saw Crouton **watching** the tournament. I sat down next to him.

"Oh, Sir Geronimo," he gushed. "There are so many knights, and they're so brave!"

Go, Grand Rat!

Go, Measly Marvin!

TELL ME, WHAT IS YOUR WISH?

Crouton and I spent the entire afternoon watching the tournament. Then DUSK fell.

"Tonight is a special night," I explained to Crouton. "It's the night of the shooting stars. You can wish upon a star. Tell me, little one, is there something you dream of?"

He blushed and shook his head.

"There's nothing?" I asked. "You can tell me."

"I do have one great dream," he whispered. "But it's an IMPOSSIBLE dream!"

"Oh, no dream is impossible!" I told him. "Tell me your dream and I promise I'll try to make it come true."

"I . . . ahem . . . I . . ." he whispered. "I want to take part in the tournament!"

"Well, as far as I know, the first things you need to have are a **horse** and a **sword**," I said.

Crouton lowered his head **SADLY**.

"I could never afford a horse," he said.

I opened my satchel. I took out the **GOLD COIN** Professor von Volt had given me.

"With this coin, you can get yourself the best horse in **Britannia**!" I said as I handed it to Crouton.

"Really?" Crouton asked in surprise. "Thank you, Sir Geronimo!"

I reached in my satchel again.

"And then, dear Crouton, you can use this **silver coin** to buy a sword."

"Thank you, Sir Geronimo, but I already found a sword," he said. "It's wedged in a rock."

"Stuck in a rock?" I asked, disbelieving.

He clasped my paw and led me to the **TOWN SQUARE**.

PAWS OFF THE SWORD!

"Here's the sword!" Crouton squeaked.

I saw a SHINING blade wedged in a rock. Little Crouton grabbed it with both little paws and lifted it above his head proudly.

"Hey, you!" someone grunted. "Where did you get that sword?"

It was Flea Flicker Junior. He grabbed Crouton's sword.

"It's . . . it's . . . it's Excalibur!" he shouted excitedly. "Hey, everyone. Come look! Get ready to meet and crown the new king of Britannia!"

I took a step forward.

"Ahem . . . Sir Flea Flicker Junior, the sword actually belongs to little Crouton," I said. "He's the mouse who DREW it from the stone."

MIDDLE AGES

EXCALIBUR

Excalibur is the legendary sword of King Arthur. Some believe the sword was embedded in a stone and could only be removed by the true king of Britain. No one knows if Excalibur ever really existed, but there really is a medieval sword wedged in a rock in St. Galgano Church in Tuscany, Italy!

Flea Flicker Junior grunted contemptuously.

"IMPOSSIBLE!" he scoffed. "I wouldn't believe it even if I saw it! And anyway, I have the sword now, and I'm keeping it. PAWS OFF!"

Sir Flea Flicker pushed through the crowd.

"My son!" he exclaimed. "You finally did something right! Great news: The tournament's over. My son has the *Sword from the Stone* and will be king of Britannia!"

Trap, Thea, Benjamin, Professor von Volt, and I stood by Crouton.

"The sword belongs to Crouton!" the professor said firmly.

All the knights crowded around the sword.

"Is it true?" they murmured. "Is it really Excalibur?"

"Someone took it out of the **STONE**!"

"Yes, it was a tiny servant. . . ."

"No, it was Flea Flicker Junior. . . ."

"At least that's what he says. . . ."

"I can't see him as **KING**. . . ."

"But no one saw him pull the **SWORD** out of the stone. . . ."

"I think this is just a prank. . . ."

Suddenly, the great **Merlin** appeared. He made a sign asking for **SILENCE**.

"Knights of Britannia, do you want a king?" he asked. "If you do, the **SWORD** will choose him."

The crowd gathered in the square. At the center of the square was a massive dark granite stone.

Merlin read the words carved in the stone:

THE MOUSE WHO EXTRACTS THIS SWORD SHALL BECOME THE RIGHTFUL KING OF BRITANNIA

"Give me Excalibur!" Merlin ordered

Flea Flicker Junior.

The mouse handed over the sword **reluctantly**.

Merlin put it back in the stone.

Flea Flicker Junior stepped up to the sword.

"Mooooove!" he ordered those in his way. "In just a moment, I'll be king!"

He grabbed the **hilt** of the sword and pulled with all his **might**. He pulled and pulled and pulled . . . but nothing happened!

"Pull, pull, pull!" his father squeaked. "Come on, Son, **puuuuuuuull**!"

Flea Flicker Junior dried his sweat-soaked whiskers.

"I can't, Daddy," he **sobbed**. "I really can't!"

"Step aside," Sir Flea Flicker said. "I'll show you how to do it!"

Panting, he pulled and

pulled and pulled . . . but the sword didn't **BUDGE** an inch.

"I want to try!" one of the knights shouted.

One after another, all the knights tried to extract the sword.

Sylvester Strongmouse of Stalwart, the strongest knight in Britannia, tried to extract the sword, but it didn't budge an inch!

Robert Roundmouse of Stoutville, the roundest knight, tried next. But in spite of his

weight, the sword didn't budge an inch!

Wilson Wisemouse of Wisdomshire, the oldest of the knights, also tried. But in spite of his wisdom, the sword didn't budge an inch!

Finally, *Richard Reekrat of Stinkonia* tried as well. Because of his odor, they left him for last. And you guessed it — the sword didn't budge an inch!

When everyone had stepped aside, disappointed, we heard a LITTLE voice.

"Can I try, too?" Crouton asked.

Sir Flea Flicker and his son laughed.

"Look here," Sir Flea Flicker **SCOFFED**. "It's Crouton the servant."

I took a step forward.

"**Let him try!**" I said firmly.

"Sure, let him try," Flea Flicker Junior sneered. "I could use a good **laugh**!"

THE SWORD THAT SINGS

I walked with Crouton to the center of the square. He took a few **timid** steps toward the stone where the sword was **WEDGED**. When he got to the stone, he hesitated and turned toward me.

"Go on, little one," I encouraged him. "It's your turn. You can do it!"

He grasped the hilt of the sword, and . . . he pulled the sword out of the stone EFFORTLESSLY.

"Oooooooooooooooooooh!" the crowd gasped.

A ray of moonlight pierced the clouds.

The sword sang **SWEETLY**:

"I am the Sword in the Stone,
And you are the heir to the throne.
The King of Britannia you'll be,
This is my solemn decree!"

"It's a trick!" Flea Flicker Junior shouted. "He's just a servant, so it doesn't COUNT! It's a trick!"

"Yes, yes!" the crowd shouted. "It must be one of Merlin's tricks!"

"The magician's paw must be in it!"

Crouton placed the SWORD back in the STONE. Then he took it out again and raised it over his head so that everyone could see. This time, there was no doubt. Merlin made a solemn gesture and raised his arms to the SKY.

"Hear ye, hear ye!" Merlin shouted. "Years have passed since our king Uther Pendragon left us forever. But today we are gathered here to CROWN his legitimate heir: his son, Arthur. Long live Britannia's new king! Long live **KING ARTHUR**!"

The crowd knelt down on the ground.

"Long live the new King of Britannia!"

Excalibur!

they all shouted. "Long live King Arthur!"

The sword blazed and the crowd chanted:

"Ar-thur! Ar-thur! Long live King Arthur!"

The little mouselet with the blonde braids gazed at Crouton — that is, Arthur — with adoring eyes.

Arthur blushed **shyly**.

"My lady!" he greeted her.

She gave him her arm, and the two walked toward the castle, gazing into each other's eyes.

"Ah, Maiden Guinevere and little **ARTHUR** look so cute together. . . ." I heard some gossipers whisper.

Merlin smiled with satisfaction.

"That was the treasure hidden in the castle: a great king. **KING ARTHUR!**"

gazing into each other's eyes . . . . . Guinevere and Arthur . . . gazing into each other's eyes

The Knights of the Round Table

According to legend, King Arthur was the secret son of the King of Britain, Uther Pendragon, and Lady Igraine, duchess of Tintagel. His half sister was Morgan le Fay. When King Pendragon died, Merlin the magician hid little Arthur in a faraway castle to protect him. When Arthur was ready to ascend the throne, Merlin revealed that he was the true king through the Sword in the Stone. Guinevere, daughter of King Leodegrance, married Arthur. Under the sage rule of King Arthur, Britain fought off the Saxon invaders. Finally, Merlin gave King Arthur one final mission: to find the Holy Grail. Supposedly, the cup held the cure to many ailments and it bestowed its owner with great wisdom. King Arthur gathered the most valiant knights around his Round Table, which was designed without a head to signify that all who sat at the table shared an equal status. He then asked for their help locating the Holy Grail. According to the legend, no one knows for sure if Arthur or his knights ever found it.

A New King and Queen

Suddenly, Professor von Volt ran up to me, panting and **OUT OF BREATH**.

"Geronimo, where have you been?" he asked. "I've been looking for you. We have to leave immediately. The **MOUSE MOVER 3000**'s batteries are almost out of power! If we don't leave soon, we may have to stay here **FOREVER**!"

"Will little Crouton be okay?" I asked Merlin, **concerned** for my young friend.

"Yes, dear *friend*," he replied. "I will make it my responsibility to advise him and to make him a good king.

"I do think the castle will need a new name, though.

The future king and queen

Flea Flicker Castle is a **horrible** name. I'll advise him to call it . . . **CAMELOT**! I think Camelot will soon have a new queen, Guinevere, that sweet little mouselet."

Professor von Volt smiled.

"Arthur, Guinevere, Camelot . . . **GOOD**!" he said. "Now everything makes sense."

Merlin raised his paw to bid us farewell.

"I won't forget you, **travelers from afar**!" he said.

We climbed aboard the Mouse Mover 3000.

"**Ready?**" squeaked Professor von Volt. "**Goooooooooo!**"

The time machine jolted.

BANGGGGGGGGGGGGGGGGG!!!

Soon we were back in New Mouse City.

Ah, it felt so good to be home!

I Give You My Word . . .

We found ourselves back in Professor von Volt's laboratory. The door opened and my friends and I climbed out of the time machine. Ah, HOME SWEET HOME!

I couldn't wait to get home and take a warm, cheddar-scented bath.

"Oh, wait!" Trap yelled. "I left my bag on the ship! Geronimo, can you get it for me? I'm late for an APPOINTMENT!"

"An appointment?" I grumbled as I climbed back inside the Mouse Mover 3000, whose batteries were charging. "When did you have time to make an APPOINTMENT while the rest of us were busy traveling through time? This better not be another one of your tricks, Trap!"

"Who, me? Do **tricks**?" Trap asked. "Be real, Geronimo. I'm the most **serious** mouse of all time! You're so **SUSPICIOUS**. It's not good for your **HEALTH**, you know? Anyway, gotta go! See you later, alligator!"

With that, he dashed out the door. As he was running out, he **TRIPPED** on something on the floor. It was the **remote control** for the **MOUSE MOVER 3000**.

Suddenly, the Mouse Mover 3000 began to **HUM**, and the door closed with a bang. This time, I knew what was happening. So I quickly buckled my seat belt and inserted the earplugs. The time machine filled with

a **BLUE** fog and began rotating ***faster*** and ***faster***! Where was I going? I didn't know. But I wasn't worried. In fact, I was excited about traveling through time **again**. Who knew what adventure I might find!

Maybe I would end up in **ancient Greece**, where I would chat with great philosophers like PLATO and ARISTOTLE. Or maybe I would find myself in ancient Rome, where I could take part in a chariot race in the Coliseum. Or perhaps I would travel to the year 1492 to see Christopher Columbus set foot in America!

Where would the Mouse Mover 3000 take me?

WHERE? WHERE? WHERE?????????????

I held on tight and —

BANGGGGGGGGGGGGG!

The time machine came to a sudden **stop**. I had a feeling I was about to have another WHISKER-LICKING-GOOD adventure!

I give you my word that whatever happens on my journey, I'll be sure to write about it . . . **someday**!

Until then, farewell, **dear mouse friends**!

TRAVEL JOURNAL

Dear rodent friends,

I hope you have enjoyed reading all about my adventures during my journey through time. To keep the memories from fading, I wrote this very special travel journal just for you. It's full of **definitions**, **MAPS**, and **FUN FACTS**.

Learn about dinosaur discoveries around the world, the Egyptian calendar, and the secrets of medieval castle construction. You'll find it's like taking off on another fabumouse journey through time!

Geronimo Stilton

PREHISTORY

PREHISTORY MINI DICTIONARY

bird: A warm-blooded animal with two legs, wings, feathers, and a beak. The oldest known bird is Archaeopteryx, which lived in the Late Jurassic period around 150 million years ago.

carnivore: An animal that eats meat.

egg: An oval or round object that contains a baby bird, reptile, fish, or insect. It is produced by the female member of these species to protect their young as they develop. Dinosaurs laid eggs in nests. The largest dinosaur eggs were as big as eighteen or nineteen inches long, while the smallest were the size of tennis balls.

family: A group of living things that are related to each other. Donkeys and mules are members of the horse family.

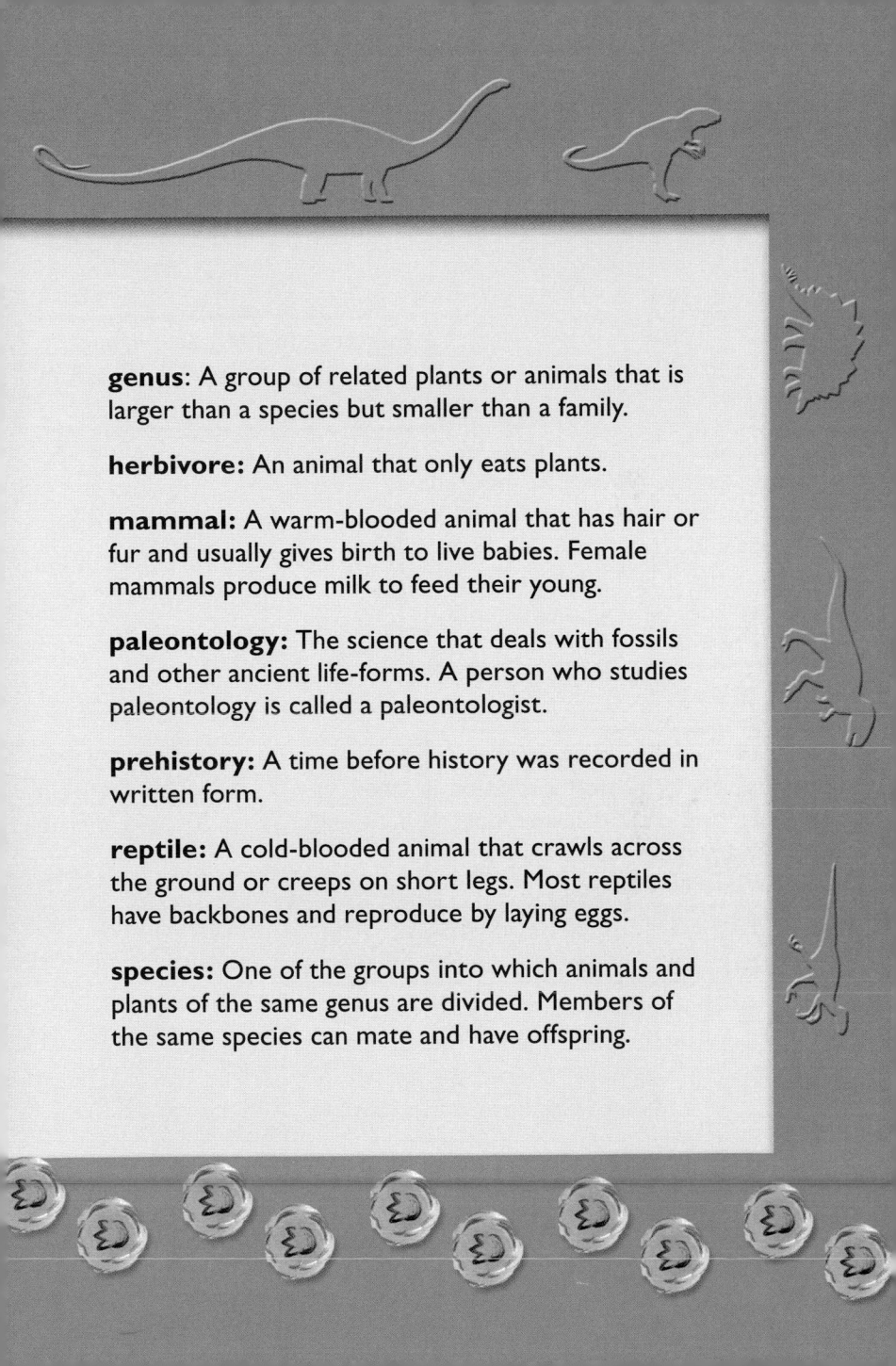

genus: A group of related plants or animals that is larger than a species but smaller than a family.

herbivore: An animal that only eats plants.

mammal: A warm-blooded animal that has hair or fur and usually gives birth to live babies. Female mammals produce milk to feed their young.

paleontology: The science that deals with fossils and other ancient life-forms. A person who studies paleontology is called a paleontologist.

prehistory: A time before history was recorded in written form.

reptile: A cold-blooded animal that crawls across the ground or creeps on short legs. Most reptiles have backbones and reproduce by laying eggs.

species: One of the groups into which animals and plants of the same genus are divided. Members of the same species can mate and have offspring.

DINOSAURS AROUND THE WORLD

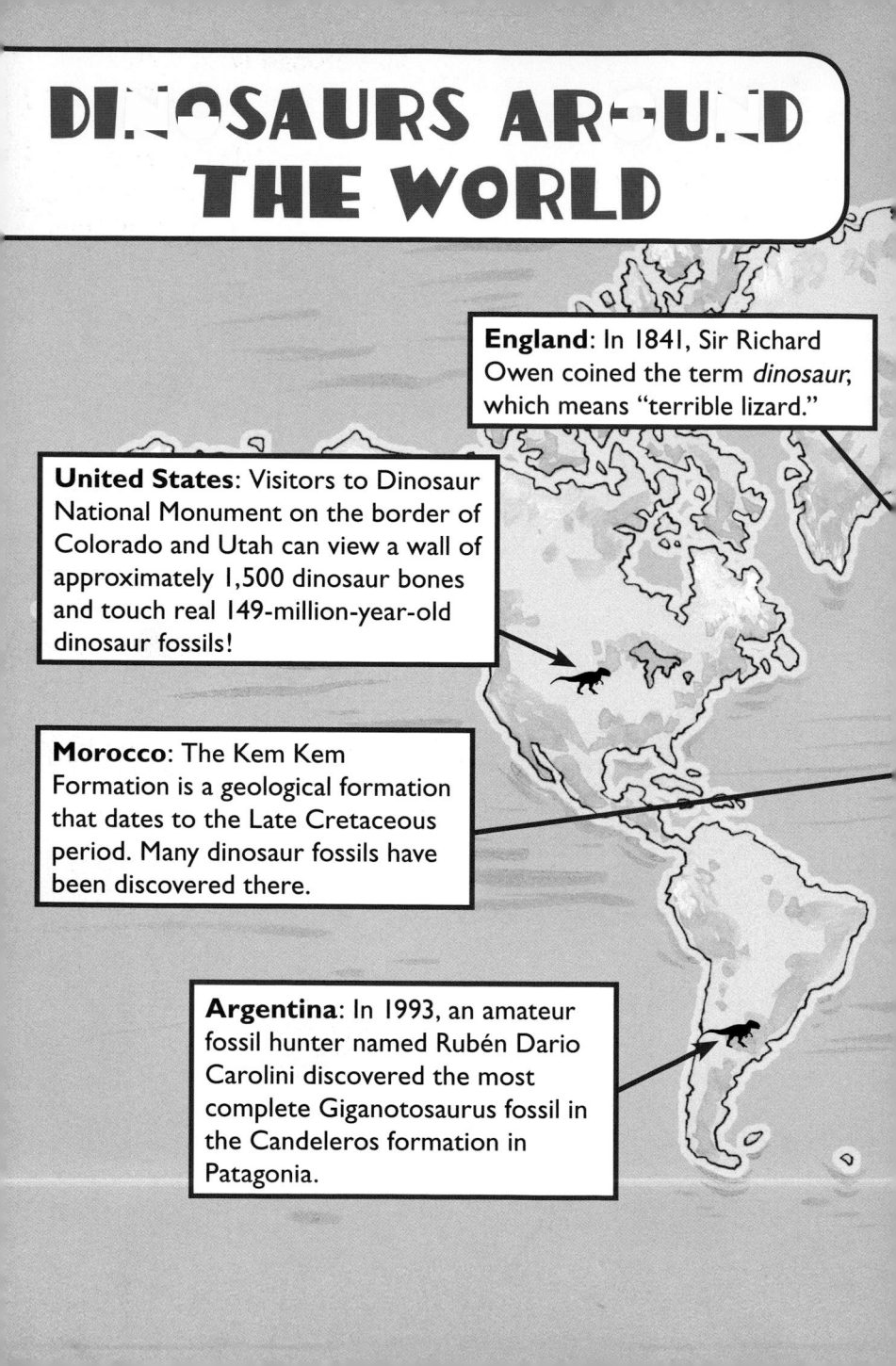

England: In 1841, Sir Richard Owen coined the term *dinosaur*, which means "terrible lizard."

United States: Visitors to Dinosaur National Monument on the border of Colorado and Utah can view a wall of approximately 1,500 dinosaur bones and touch real 149-million-year-old dinosaur fossils!

Morocco: The Kem Kem Formation is a geological formation that dates to the Late Cretaceous period. Many dinosaur fossils have been discovered there.

Argentina: In 1993, an amateur fossil hunter named Rubén Dario Carolini discovered the most complete Giganotosaurus fossil in the Candeleros formation in Patagonia.

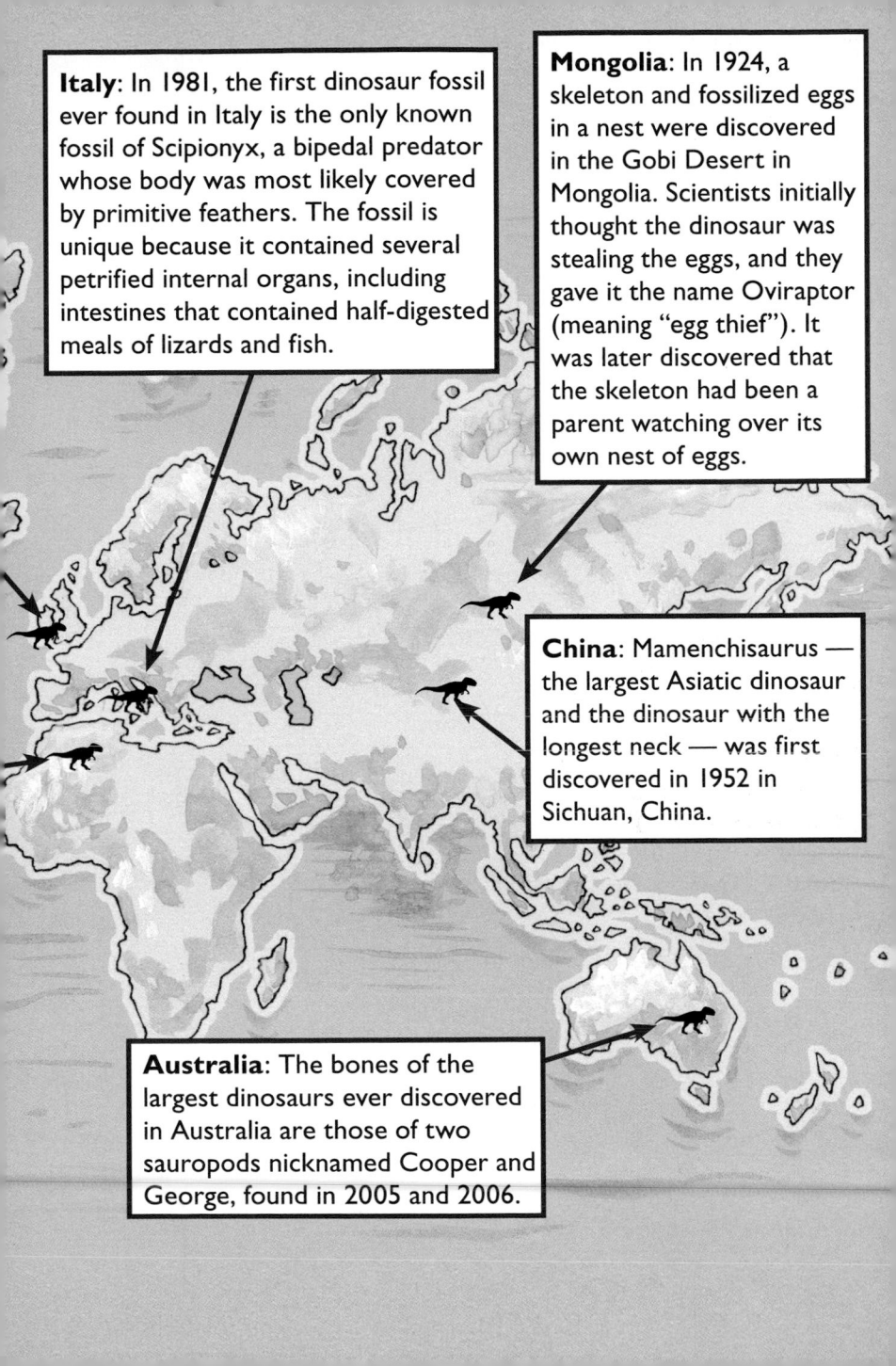
Italy: In 1981, the first dinosaur fossil ever found in Italy is the only known fossil of Scipionyx, a bipedal predator whose body was most likely covered by primitive feathers. The fossil is unique because it contained several petrified internal organs, including intestines that contained half-digested meals of lizards and fish.
Mongolia: In 1924, a skeleton and fossilized eggs in a nest were discovered in the Gobi Desert in Mongolia. Scientists initially thought the dinosaur was stealing the eggs, and they gave it the name Oviraptor (meaning "egg thief"). It was later discovered that the skeleton had been a parent watching over its own nest of eggs.
China: Mamenchisaurus — the largest Asiatic dinosaur and the dinosaur with the longest neck — was first discovered in 1952 in Sichuan, China.
Australia: The bones of the largest dinosaurs ever discovered in Australia are those of two sauropods nicknamed Cooper and George, found in 2005 and 2006.

Prehistory Fun Facts

The dinosaur that . . .

Was the fastest:	Dromiceiomimus could run at a speed of around thirty-seven miles per hour.
Was the heaviest:	Argentinosaurus weighed around eighty tons.
Was the tallest:	Sauroposeidon's head could reach fifty-seven feet in height.
Had the longest neck:	Mamenchisaurus's neck made up half its length.
Had the longest tail:	Diplodocus's tail was up to forty-five feet long.
Had the longest name:	Micropachycephalosaurus
Was the first discovered:	Megalosaurus was discovered and named in 1824.

EGYPT

EGYPT MINI DICTIONARY

amulet: A charm or object that is said to have magical powers that protect the owner.

archaeology: The study of the distant past, which often involves digging up old buildings, objects, and bones and examining them carefully.

cubit: An ancient form of measurement based on the length of the forearm, measured from the elbow to the tip of the middle finger. Usually equal to about eighteen to twenty inches (forty-six to fifty-two centimeters).

deben: An ancient Egyptian stone used as a measurement for weight. Copper deben weighed about 13.6 grams each, while gold deben weighed about 23.7 grams each. Deben could be used as currency in exchange for goods and services.

Egyptology: The study of the civilization of ancient Egypt.

hieroglyphics: A system of writing used by ancient Egyptians, made up of pictures and symbols that stand for words.

mastaba: An Egyptian tomb that is oblong-shaped with sloping sides and a flat roof, like the base of a pyramid.

necropolis: A place dedicated to burials and worship of the dead.

obelisk: An upright four-sided pillar built out of one piece of stone that gradually tapers as it rises and ends in a pyramid on top. It was usually decorated with inscriptions.

papyrus: A tall water plant that grows in northern Africa and southern Europe. Ancient Egyptians used the stems of the plant to make writing paper.

pyramid: An ancient Egyptian stone monument where pharaohs and their treasures were buried.

Egyptian Calendar

The Egyptian year was made up of 365 days and had three seasons made up of four months each:

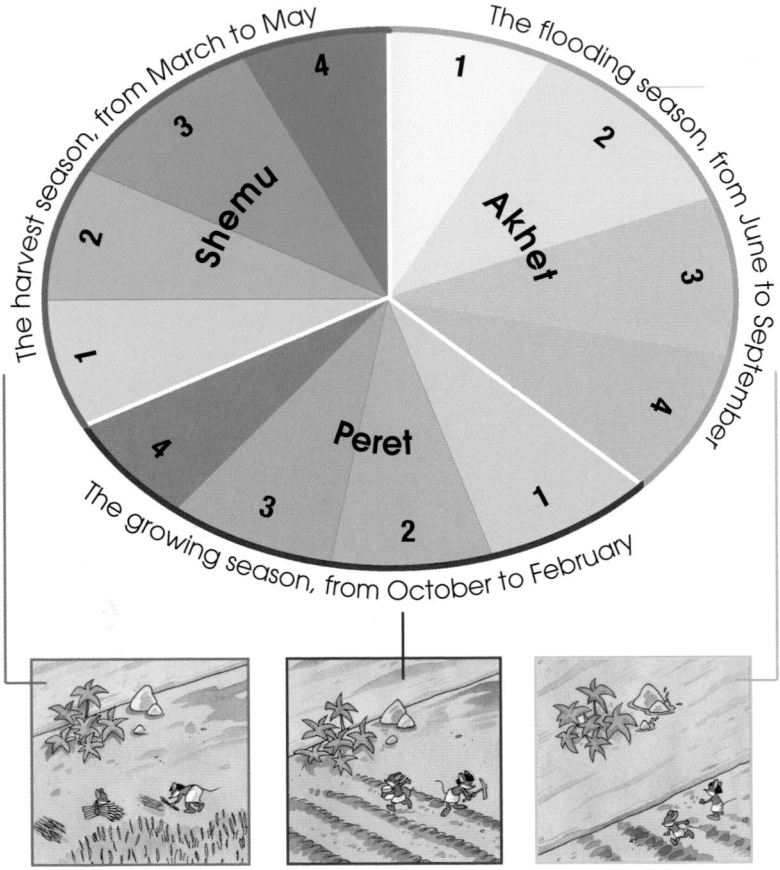

Every month was made up of thirty days, divided into three weeks of ten days each.

New Year's Day fell in mid-July, which is when the waters of the Nile River began to rise rapidly. It was preceded by five days of great festivities to honor the birth of:

ISIS
goddess of nature and magic

HORUS
god of war and hunting

NEPHTHYS
goddess of death

OSIRIS
god of the afterlife

SET
god of the desert

Egypt Fun Facts

The oldest pyramid . . .
is the Pyramid of Djoser in the Sahara desert in Egypt, northwest of the city of Memphis. It was built during the twenty-seventh century BC for the pharaoh Djoser and was originally 203 feet tall.

The oldest obelisk . . .
is that of Senusret in Heliopolis. It is 67 feet tall, weighs 120 tons (240,000 pounds), and is made of red granite.

The tallest obelisk . . .
is that of Tuthmosis III. Today it stands in the Piazza San Giovanni in Laterano, Rome, where it has been since 1588. It is 105 feet tall.

The oldest hieroglyphs . . .
come from Abydos, 300 miles south of Cairo. The symbols were found on pieces of pottery, bone and ivory tags, and clay seal impressions that are dated between 3400 and 3200 BC.

MIDDLE
AGES

MIDDLE AGES MINI DICTIONARY

amanuensis: A medieval monk or servant whose job it was to write books from dictation by hand and illustrate them with miniature drawings.

arrow slit: A thin vertical cutout opening in a castle wall that archers can use to launch arrows at invading forces. Also called an *arrow loop* or *loop hole*.

coronation: The ceremony in which a king, queen, or other ruler is crowned.

jester: A professional joker or entertainer in medieval courts.

joust: A competition between two knights on horseback with lances.

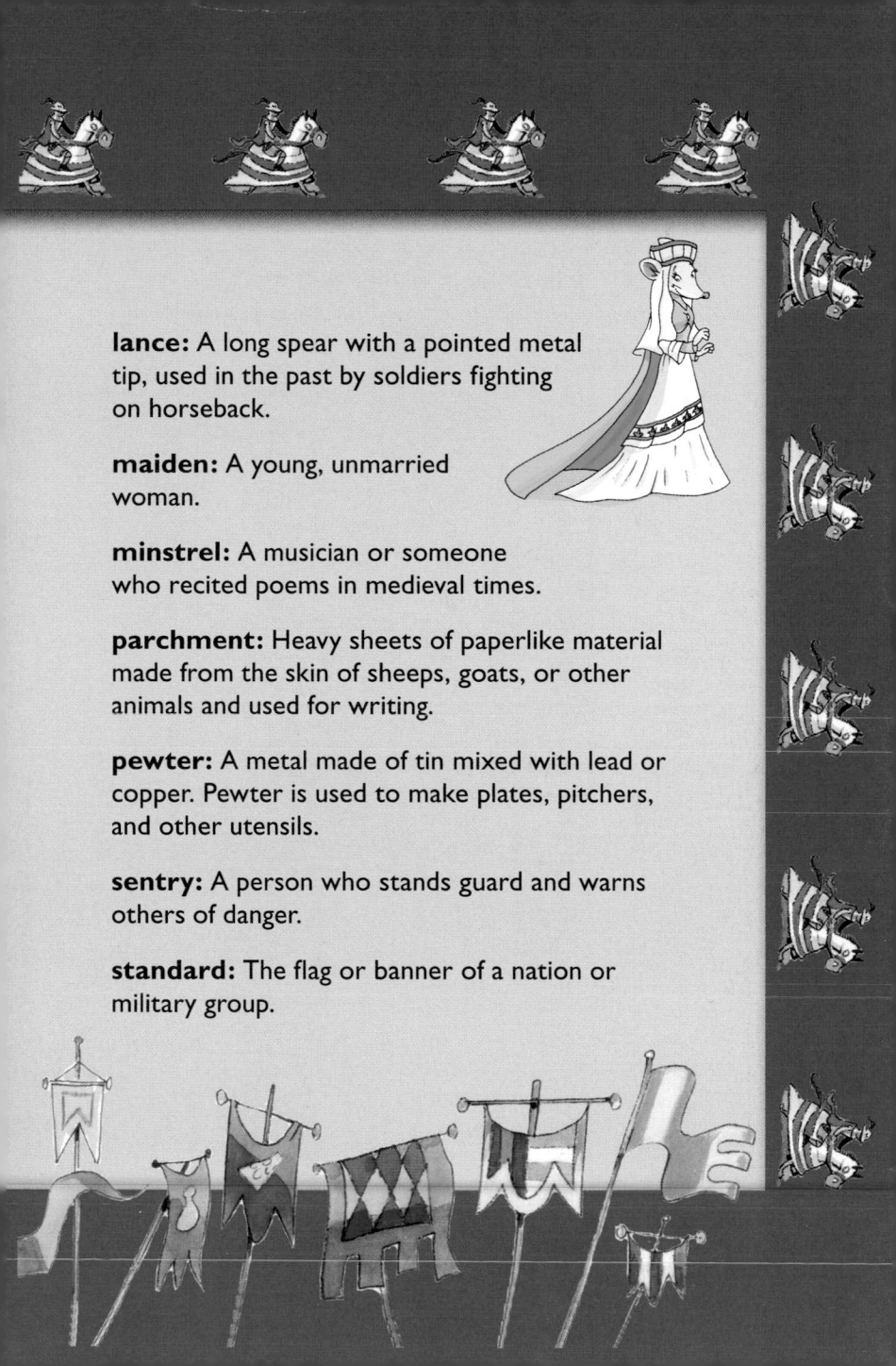

lance: A long spear with a pointed metal tip, used in the past by soldiers fighting on horseback.

maiden: A young, unmarried woman.

minstrel: A musician or someone who recited poems in medieval times.

parchment: Heavy sheets of paperlike material made from the skin of sheeps, goats, or other animals and used for writing.

pewter: A metal made of tin mixed with lead or copper. Pewter is used to make plates, pitchers, and other utensils.

sentry: A person who stands guard and warns others of danger.

standard: The flag or banner of a nation or military group.

The Secrets of the Castle

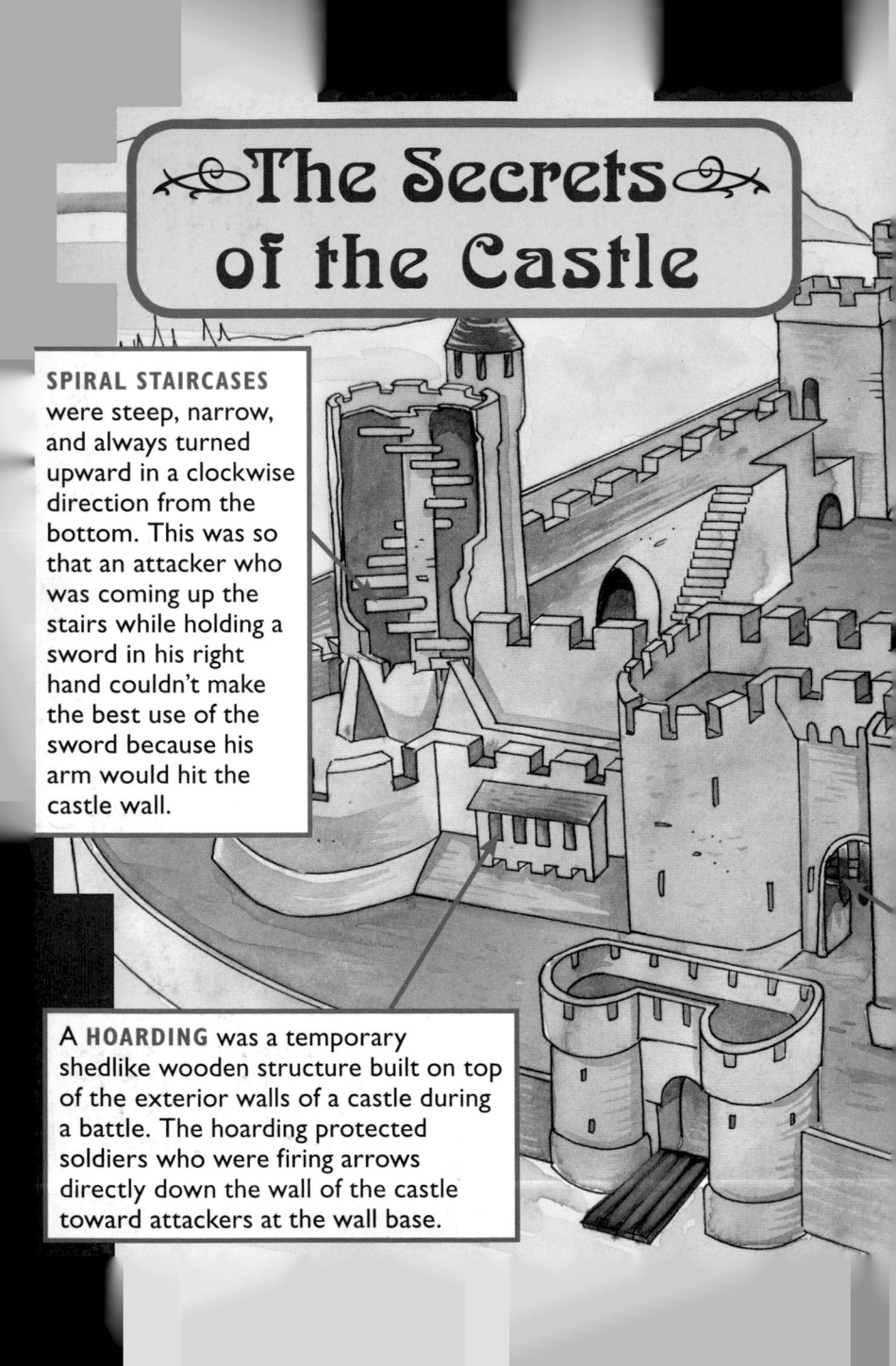

SPIRAL STAIRCASES were steep, narrow, and always turned upward in a clockwise direction from the bottom. This was so that an attacker who was coming up the stairs while holding a sword in his right hand couldn't make the best use of the sword because his arm would hit the castle wall.

A **HOARDING** was a temporary shedlike wooden structure built on top of the exterior walls of a castle during a battle. The hoarding protected soldiers who were firing arrows directly down the wall of the castle toward attackers at the wall base.

The **KEEP** was a remote, fortified tower built within the castle that served as a refuge of last resort if an enemy overtook the rest of the castle.
A **PORTCULLIS** was a latticed grille made of wood or metal that was mounted in vertical grooves in the castle walls. It could be raised or lowered quickly using chains or ropes attached to a winch in order to securely close off the castle during an attack.
The **EXTERIOR WALLS** that surrounded the castle often had walkways along the top to allow defenders to move quickly around the castle.

Middle Ages Fun Facts

- The largest medieval castle in central Europe is the **Spiš Castle** in eastern Slovakia, which is now partially in ruins.
- It usually took around **seven to twelve years** to build a medieval castle. Some larger castles, like the Tower of London, were rebuilt and added on to for hundreds of years.
- **Château Gaillard** is a medieval castle in Normandy, France, that was built by Richard the Lionheart beginning in 1196. Remarkably, the castle was constructed in just two years.
- The oldest standing castle in Europe is part of the **Château de Doué-la-Fontaine** in western France. The castle is believed to have been the first European castle built out of stone in around 950.

IN WHICH HISTORICAL PERIOD WOULD YOU HAVE LIVED?

QUIZ

1 At the end of dinner, which dessert would you choose?

a) A pistachio ice-cream cone
b) An almond and honey pastry
c) A slice of wild berry pie

2 What do you do if you don't agree with someone else's opinion?

a) You get angry.
b) You try to find a compromise.
c) You make your point of view known through a conversation.

3 What are your favorite subjects?

a) History and geography
b) Math and geometry
c) English and drawing

4 Which color do you like the most?

a) Green
b) Yellow
c) Blue

5 **Which of these places would you most like to visit?**

a) A tropical forest
b) The desert
c) An abandoned castle

6 **What profession interests you the most?**

a) Geologist (someone who studies the earth's physical structure, especially soil and rocks)
b) Archeologist (someone who studies the past, often by digging up and examining the remains of old buildings, objects, and bones)
c) Philologist (someone who studies literature, history, and classic languages)

7 **Which pet would you most like to have?**

a) A prehistoric fish
b) A cat
c) A horse

8 **What's your favorite way to spend an afternoon with a friend?**

a) Flying a kite at the park
b) Playing at home
c) Drawing or writing stories together

9 Which type of house would you like most?

a) A tree house
b) A palace
c) A small country home

10 Where would you most like to live?

a) At the foot of a mountain
b) Near a river
c) On a small, rolling hill

11 If you were invited to a birthday party, what would you wear?

a) Comfortable everyday clothes
b) Something fun and fancy
c) Anything, as long as it matches

In what period would you have lived?

HERE ARE THE RESULTS...

Prehistoric

If you answered **A** to most questions, you are adventurous and can always get out of a tricky situation. You probably would have most liked living in the prehistoric era.

Egyptian

If you answered **B** to most of the questions, you are detail-oriented, patient, and calm, and you solve problems with a lot of thought and care. You probably would have most liked living in ancient Egypt.

Medieval

If you answered **C** to most of the questions, you have a vivid imagination, but you are also a rational thinker. You probably would have most liked living in the Middle Ages, where you would have been a faithful advisor to the king.

Be sure to read all my adventures in the Kingdom of Fantasy!

THE KINGDOM OF FANTASY

THE QUEST FOR PARADISE:
THE RETURN TO THE KINGDOM OF FANTASY

THE AMAZING VOYAGE:
THE THIRD ADVENTURE IN THE KINGDOM OF FANTASY

THE DRAGON PROPHECY:
THE FOURTH ADVENTURE IN THE KINGDOM OF FANTASY

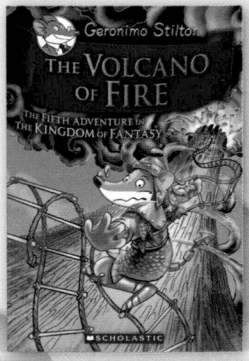

THE VOLCANO OF FIRE:
THE FIFTH ADVENTURE IN THE KINGDOM OF FANTASY

Don't miss any of my other fabumouse adventures!

#1 Lost Treasure of the Emerald Eye

#2 The Curse of the Cheese Pyramid

#3 Cat and Mouse in a Haunted House

#4 I'm Too Fond of My Fur!

#5 Four Mice Deep in the Jungle

#6 Paws Off, Cheddarface!

#7 Red Pizzas for a Blue Count

#8 Attack of the Bandit Cats

#9 A Fabumouse Vacation for Geronimo

#10 All Because of a Cup of Coffee

#11 It's Halloween, You 'Fraidy Mouse!

#12 Merry Christmas, Geronimo!

#13 The Phantom of the Subway

#14 The Temple of the Ruby of Fire

#15 The Mona Mousa Code

#16 A Cheese-Colored Camper

#17 Watch Your Whiskers, Stilton!

#18 Shipwreck on the Pirate Islands

#19 My Name Is Stilton, Geronimo Stilton

#20 Surf's Up, Geronimo!

#21 The Wild, Wild West

#22 The Secret of Cacklefur Castle

A Christmas Tale

#23 Valentine's Day Disaster

#24 Field Trip to Niagara Falls

#25 The Search for Sunken Treasure

#26 The Mummy with No Name

#27 The Christmas Toy Factory

#28 Wedding Crasher

#29 Down and Out Down Under

#30 The Mouse Island Marathon

#31 The Mysterious Cheese Thief

Christmas Catastrophe

#32 Valley of the Giant Skeletons

#33 Geronimo and the Gold Medal Mystery

#34 Geronimo Stilton, Secret Agent

#35 A Very Merry Christmas

#36 Geronimo's Valentine

#37 The Race Across America

#38 A Fabumouse School Adventure

#39 Singing Sensation

#40 The Karate Mouse

#41 Mighty Mount Kilimanjaro

#42 The Peculiar Pumpkin Thief

#43 I'm Not a Supermouse!

#44 The Giant Diamond Robbery

#45 Save the White Whale!

#46 The Haunted Castle

#47 Run for the Hills, Geronimo!

#48 The Mystery in Venice

#49 The Way of the Samurai

#50 This Hotel Is Haunted

#51 The Enormouse Pearl Heist

#52 Mouse in Space!

#53 Rumble in the Jungle

#54 Get into Gear, Stilton!

#55 The Golden Statue Plot

#56 Flight of the Red Bandit

The Hunt for the Golden Book

Check out these very special editions featuring me and the Thea Sisters!

THE JOURNEY TO ATLANTIS

THE SECRET OF THE FAIRIES

Don't miss these exciting Thea Sisters adventures!

Thea Stilton and the Dragon's Code

Thea Stilton and the Mountain of Fire

Thea Stilton and the Ghost of the Shipwreck

Thea Stilton and the Secret City

Thea Stilton and the Mystery in Paris

Thea Stilton and the Cherry Blossom Adventure

Thea Stilton and the Star Castaways

Thea Stilton: Big Trouble in the Big Apple

Thea Stilton and the Ice Treasure

Thea Stilton and the Secret of the Old Castle

Thea Stilton and the Blue Scarab Hunt

Thea Stilton and the Prince's Emerald

Thea Stilton and the Mystery on the Orient Express

Thea Stilton and the Dancing Shadows

Thea Stilton and the Legend of the Fire Flowers

Thea Stilton and the Spanish Dance Mission

Thea Stilton and the Journey to the Lion's Den

Thea Stilton and the Great Tulip Heist

Meet GERONIMO STILTONOOT

He is a cavemouse—Geronimo Stilton's ancient ancestor! He runs the stone newspaper in the prehistoric village of Old Mouse City. From dealing with dinosaurs to dodging meteorites, his life in the Stone Age is full of adventure!

#1 The Stone of Fire

#2 Watch Your Tail!

#3 Help, I'm in Hot Lava!

#4 The Fast and the Frozen

#5 The Great Mouse Race